喚醒你的英文語感！

Get a Feel for English !

學校沒教的英文口語

從硬邦邦的文法句子，到老外在說的自然英文！

資深美籍總編幫你

修正呆板英文

作者 **David Katz**

活、旅遊、面試、職場英文

What do you do for fun?

WHAT IS YOUR HOBBY?

Preface to the Second Edition

After a decade upturned by a devastating tsunami, political turmoil, and a global pandemic, it's comforting to know that some things never change. In the ten years since the first edition of this book was published, English language textbooks continue to be written and the language they contain continues to be safe, stilted, and stultifying.

Watching as my two children work their way through years of local elementary and junior high school English textbooks has only deepened my ambivalence about the curriculum. As a writer of language learning materials, I genuinely appreciate the carefully constructed lessons, the imaginative use of multimedia, and the flashes of true creativity that shine through in the exercises and artwork. As a lover of the English language, I mourn the lifelessness of the prose. The reading passages and dialogs exist primarily to model grammatical structures, not natural speech.

Ten years from now, the situation may have changed. Most kids in Taiwan now have some access to authentic English media. Whether it's English language music, video games, or YouTube channels, "the real thing" is never more than a tap away. My children's teachers encourage their students to take advantage of these resources. I hope that the writers and gatekeepers who are creating the next versions of their textbooks are able to do so as well. Until that time arrives, books like this one will continue to be necessary for anyone who wants to make the English they use a little more natural.

This second edition makes some minor revisions and additions to the main body of the text. It also features an entirely new section of phrases that are formed from very common words. This section was inspired by the widespread tendency among some English learners to fixate on the acquisition of esoteric vocabulary at the expense of learning common phrases that are almost always much more useful.

It's wrong to view the vast and varied vocabulary of English as an impediment to learning the language. The simple fact of the matter is that almost all of the hundreds of thousands of English words are superfluous. Just 2,000 words account for about 80% of all the words most people encounter in their daily lives. Even with only a hundred words, you can read about half of everything.

This seems surprising until you stop to consider the thousands of very useful expressions that are formed by combining just a few of those one hundred most common words. Everyone knows what "on" and "it" mean, but when you can throw a casual "on it" (see page 22) into your next conversation, you'll know you've taken your English to the next level. There's no need to memorize the dictionary to get there.

The purpose of this new section is to introduce a representative sample of those common expressions, but more importantly to suggest a mode of learning that emphasizes noticing, association, and mastery rather than grueling feats of memorization. Picking up little phrases like these is an easy and efficient way to expand your vocabulary—and you can do it just like that.

David Katz

二版序

在經歷了毀滅性海嘯、政治動盪和全球疫情大流行的十年後，令人欣慰的是，有些事情永遠不會改變。自本書第一版出版後十年來，市面上各種英語教科書相繼不斷，且其中所包含的文字語言持續走著安全、生硬和枯燥的路線。

這些年來看著我的兩個孩子在本地小學和中學努力地就著英語教科書學習，在在加深我對課程的矛盾心理。作為一名語言學習素材的作者，我非常感謝精心設計的課堂、富有想像力的多媒體運用，以及在練習和美勞作品中閃耀的創造力光芒；作為一個英語愛好者，我為行文寫作的呆板而哀悼。文章讀本和對話主要是為了模擬文法結構而存在，而不是自然的語言。

十年後，情況可能已經有所改變。現在台灣的大多數孩子都可以接觸到道地的英語媒體。無論是英語音樂、電玩遊戲或 YouTube 頻道，所謂「真實」，不過就在彈指之間。我家孩子的老師鼓勵學生們多多利用這些資源，而我希望正在創作下一版教科書的作家和把關者也能夠這樣做。直至那一刻來臨之前，對任何想讓自身所使用的英文稍加自然些的人而言，像本書的書籍將持續具有其必要性。

✳✳

本次改版針對主文做了若干小修改和增補，其中「暖身篇」是一大亮點，這段全新內容收錄的詞語是由極其常見的單字所組成，靈感來自一些英語學習者普遍存在的現象——傾向專注於獲得深奧的詞彙，而犧牲了學習實用好幾倍的常用短語。

　　將大量而多樣化的英語詞彙視爲學習語言的障礙是錯誤的。事實上顯而易見地，成千上萬的英語單字幾乎是多餘的。大多數人在日常生活裡遇到的所有單字中，八成只有兩千個單字。即使只具備一百個字的字彙量，您也可以閱讀大半的內容。

　　這似乎令人驚訝，僅僅用這一百個最常見單字中的幾個來加以組合，就能形成數以千計實用的表達方式。每個人都知道 "on" 和 "it" 是什麼意思，但當您可以在下一次對話中隨意加上 "on it"（見第 22 頁）時，您就會知道自己的英語水準已經更上一層樓，而不需要背下整本字典。

　　本次新增的「暖身篇」旨在介紹這些常用說法的代表性範例，但更重要的是，提出側重於留意、聯想和熟練的學習模式，而非艱辛的背誦技巧。學習如此的短語是擴充字彙量的一種簡單而有效的方法，並且您可以輕易做到。

David Katz

本書特色

聚焦詞句一對一 Battle

老外說的跟你不一樣，究竟哪裡有問題？

琢磨語感讓口語表達更道地！

① 說法比一比

「老外說的」和「學校教的」有什麼不同？對比兩種說法，再加上作者的解說，語言的微妙差異一目了然。（學校所教的句子並沒有文法上的錯誤，只是老外不(常)會那樣使用。）

② 實境對話

以貼近生活場景的對話示範老外慣常使用的句子用法，幫助讀者進一步掌握該句的使用方式。

③ 舉一反三學起來！

以主題句為中心再向外延伸類似說法或相關語句，透過彼此互有相關性的群組學習，記憶更容易刻入腦海，同時也更不易看過即忘。

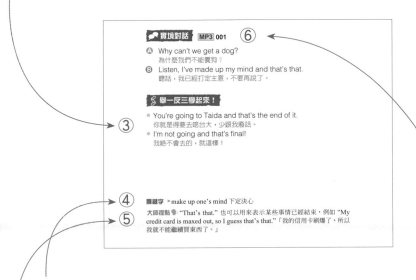

實境對話 MP3 001 ⑥

Ⓐ Why can't we get a dog?
為什麼我們不能養狗？

Ⓑ Listen, I've made up my mind and that's that.
聽話，我已經打定主意，不要再說了。

舉一反三學起來！

● You're going to Taida and that's the end of it.
你就是得要去唸台大，少跟我廢話。

● I'm not going and that's final!
我絕不會去的，就這樣！

③

④ **關鍵字** ▶ make up one's mind 下定決心

⑤ **大師提點** ➡ "That's that." 也可以用來表示某些事情已經結束，例如 "My credit card is maxed out, so I guess that's that." 「我的信用卡刷爆了，所以我就不能繼續買東西了。」

④ 關鍵字

列出該主題的常用字詞，讀者可依關鍵字群造出符合自身情境、正確又自然的句子。

⑤ 大師提點

此處為針對某些用語差異或易混淆點的提醒，引導讀者藉以將老外用字遣詞的思維方式和習慣內化。

⑥ 關於 MP3

本書「實境對話」、「舉一反三學起來！」、「關鍵字」三部分附有發音示範，MP3 音檔請刮開書內刮刮卡，上網啟用序號後即可下載聆聽使用。

網址：https://bit.ly/3d3P7te，或掃描 QR code

貝塔會員網

Chapter 1 / 口語必通篇

Part 1　基本對話必備

No Problem.

You're welcome.

What are you doing recently?

What have you been up to?

Chapter 2 / 聊天有梗篇

Could you tell me about yourself?

Chapter 3 / 吃喝玩樂篇

Part 1　用餐

Part 2　購物

Do you have any discount?

Part 3　旅行

Learning Vocabulary

Just Like That

學校教的初級詞彙＋學校教的初級詞彙

＝學校沒教的英文口語

A surprisingly large number of useful phrases can be formed by combining two or three simple English words. The resulting expressions are quick to learn and easy to remember, but that doesn't mean they themselves are simple. As Aristotle said, the whole is greater than the sum of its parts. For example:

Not + All + There = "Not all there"

Complex concepts and subtle ideas (such as being mentally unsound) can be expressed just as well using the vocabulary of a kindergartener.

透過組合兩三個簡單的英文單字，可形成數量驚人的實用短語。由此產生的表達方式易於學習和記憶，但這並不意味著這些詞語盡是平易無奇。正如亞里斯多德所言「整體大於部分之總和」。比方說：

Not + All + There = "Not all there"（比喻精神有點錯亂）

複雜的概念和晦澀難懂的詞語（例如「神智不清」一詞）也能夠使用幼稚園兒童等級的詞彙來表達。

1 That vs. That's that

 ◀◀◀ 說法比一比 ▶▶▶

學校 **That 那；那個**
That's a book. 那是一本書。

老外 **That's that.**
不要再說了。

實境對話　MP3 001

A Why can't we get a dog?
為什麼我們不能養狗？

B Listen, I've made up my mind and that's that.
聽話，我已經打定主意，不要再說了。

舉一反三學起來！

- You're going to Taida and that's the end of it.
  你就是得要去唸台大，少跟我廢話。
- I'm not going and that's final!
  我絕不會去的，就這樣！

關鍵字 ▶ make up one's mind 下定決心

大師提點 "That's that." 也可以用來表示某些事情已經結束，例如 "My credit card is maxed out, so I guess that's that." 「我的信用卡刷爆了，所以我就不能繼續買東西了。」

2 Come vs. Come again?

◄◄◄ **說法比一比** ►►►

暖身篇

學校 **Come** 來；過來
Please come here. 請過來。

老外 **Come again?**
再說一遍。

💬 實境對話 `MP3 002`

Ⓐ Come again? I didn't hear you.
　再說一遍。我剛沒聽到。
Ⓑ I asked you if you were paying attention.
　我剛問你有沒有在注意。

✍ 舉一反三學起來！

● I'm sorry, I didn't quite get that.
　對不起，我不太懂你的意思。
　notes 此說法也可指「沒聽到」。
● Sorry, I missed that.
　抱歉，我沒聽到。

關鍵字 ▶ pay attention 留神；注意

大師提點 🔊 雖然大多時候用來請別人複述某事，但是 Come again? 也可用來表達驚喜之情或不相信某事。不過，和中文一樣，在英文裡店家也會對顧客說 "Thank you. Come again."，意思是「謝謝，再來喔」，這幾種用法小心別搞混了。

15

3 All vs. All that

  ◄◄◄ 說法比一比 ►►►

 All 全部的
I want to eat all the cookies. 我想吃掉所有的餅乾。

老外 **All that**
那麼地

💬 實境對話 MP3 003

Ⓐ Did you hear about the UFO hovering over Taipei?
你有聽說台北上空有飛碟盤旋嗎？

Ⓑ Yeah, I'm not all that worried about it.
有啊，但我並沒有那麼擔心這件事。

🎵 舉一反三學起來！

● I'm not too worried about it.
我不太擔心。

● I'm not very concerned.
我不是很在意。

關鍵字 ▶ hover 盤旋；徘徊

大師提點 🗨 當表達「那麼地」時，通常都是用在否定句裡。"All that" 也可指「那些東西」，例如 "She's really into working out and all that."「她很熱衷於健身那類東西」，甚或亦可指「特別棒的」，例如 "He thinks he's all that, but he's not."「他認為自己很神，但並不是。」

4 This vs. This and that

 ◄◄◄ 說法比一比 ►►►

學校 **This** 這;這個
This is a pen. 這是一枝筆。

老外 **This and that**
各式各樣的(不重要的)事物

實境對話 MP3 004

Ⓐ What have you been up to lately?
你最近在忙什麼?

Ⓑ Oh, this and that. You?
噢,就一些有的沒的事。你呢?

舉一反三學起來!

● A: What's up? 在忙什麼?
  B: Not much. 沒啥事。
● A: How are you doing? 你好嗎?
  B: OK. Keeping busy. 還行。一直都很忙。

大師提點 "This and that" 傳達了一種隨意的感覺。(當你不想細說時也可派上用場。)假如要特別強調,你還可以說 "this, that, and the other",例如 "We were just chatting about this, that, and the other and it got so late he missed his train." 「我們顧著閒聊,結果聊太晚了,所以他就錯過了火車。」

5 Have vs. Have had it

 ◄◄◄ 說法比一比 ►►►

Have 有
I have a little brother. 我有一個弟弟。

Have had it
受夠了

實境對話　MP3 005

Ⓐ Ugh! I've had it with these damn mosquitoes!
啊！我受夠了這些該死的蚊子！

Ⓑ Nasty little suckers, aren't they?
真是討人厭的傢伙，對吧？

舉一反三學起來！

- I'm so sick of these little bloodsuckers.
  我厭倦了這些吸血的小玩意。
- I'm fed up with all these bed bugs.
  這些臭蟲真的好煩人。

關鍵字 ▶ nasty 令人討厭的、sucker 東西；令人討厭的人事物、bloodsucker 吸血動物、be fed up 感到厭煩的、bed bug 臭蟲（床蝨）

大師提點 通常 "have had it" 用來描述無法再忍受之事物，但是也可用以描述不再有效或根本沒用的東西，例如 "I think my phone has had it."「我想我的手機壞了」；或指某人／物精疲力盡、被打敗或瀕臨死亡，例如 "If we don't turn a profit soon, the company has had it."「如果我們不趕緊開始賺錢，公司就要倒了。」

6 Make vs. Make time

 ◄◄◄ **說法比一比** ►►►

學校 **Make** 做；製作
My grandma makes my clothes. 我的衣服都是奶奶做的。

老外 **Make time**
騰出時間；抽空

💬 實境對話　MP3 006

Ⓐ I don't have time to finish my chemistry homework.
我沒時間完成我的化學作業。

Ⓑ Well, you'll just have to make time for it.
嗯，你就是必須要擠出一點時間給它。

🔑 舉一反三學起來！

● Sorry, I just couldn't find the time to work on it.
對不起，我實在找不出時間處理這件事。

● I need to devote a little more time to exercising.
我需要投入多一些時間去運動。

大師提點 🗣 "Make time" 也有「快速移動（走路或駕車等）；趕路」的意思，例如 "If we want to get to the store before it closes, we really have to make time." 「如果想在商店關門前抵達，我們真的必須動作快一點。」

7 Now vs. Now and then

 ◀◀◀ 說法比一比 ▶▶▶

學校 **Now** 現在
I'm watching TV now. 我正在看電視。

老外 **Now and then**
偶爾；有時

🗨 實境對話　MP3 007

A Do you like basketball?
你喜歡籃球嗎？

B I don't play, but I watch it on TV every now and then.
我不打籃球，但我偶爾看看電視上的籃球比賽。

⑤ 舉一反三學起來！

- I shoot hoops every now and again.
  我三不五時投投籃球。
- I'll catch an NBA game every once in a while.
  我偶爾會看一下 NBA 球賽。

關鍵字 ▶ now and again 偶爾、shoot hoops 打籃球、catch 及時趕上（做某事）、once in a while 有時

大師提點 🗣 "Now" 經常與其他時間詞連用，例如 "now then"「喂（引起注意）」、"now now"「好了啦；可以了（安慰某人或提出溫和的警告）」，以及 "any time now"「隨時；很快」。

8 Say vs. You said it

 ◀◀◀ 說法比一比 ▶▶▶

學校 **Say** 說；講
Remember to say "please." 記得要說「請」。

老外 **You said it.**
真是這樣。

💬 實境對話　MP3 008

A I don't think I've had better tacos.
這是我吃過最好吃的塔可了。

B Yeah, you said it! I'm going to get a couple more.
嗯，真的！我要再去拿一些。

⚙ 舉一反三學起來！

- A: The enchiladas here are amazing! 這裡的墨西哥捲餅太讚了！
  B: I'll say. 的確如此！
- A: We should come back here all the time. 我們要常常回來。
  B: You can say that again. 你說的沒錯。

關鍵字 ▶ taco 塔可餅（墨西哥夾餅）、enchilada 安吉拉捲（墨西哥捲餅的一種）

大師提點 💬 句中帶有 "say" 的說法其涵義在很大程度上取決於主詞。試比較："Who can say?"「誰知道」、"They say"「據說」、"I can't say"「我不知道」和 "It's hard to say"「很難說」。

9 It vs. On it

  ◄◄◄ **說法比一比** ►►►

學校 **It** 它
It is an eraser. 這是橡皮擦。

老外 **On it**
處理

💬 實境對話 MP3 009

A We're going to need somebody to handle the social media accounts.
我們將需要有人來負責社交媒體帳戶。

B Don't worry. I'm on it.
別擔心。我來處理。

🎸 舉一反三學起來！

- Take it easy. I'm working on it.
別緊張。這事我在處理。
- Relax. I'll handle it.
放輕鬆。我會處理。

關鍵字 ▶ social media account 社交媒體帳戶

大師提點 🗣 如果說你 "on it"，意思是指你在積極解決問題。這只是許多包含介系詞和 "it" 的短語之一，其他還有 "in it"「麻煩大了」、"out of it"「在狀況外；昏昏沉沉」，以及 "with it"「時尚的」等。

10 How vs. How come?

 ◄◄◄ 說法比一比 ►►►

學校 **How 如何**
How do you spell apple? "Apple" 這個字怎麼拼？

老外 **How come?**
為什麼？

🗨️ **實境對話** `MP3` **010**

Ⓐ A-P-L-E.
A-P-L-E。
Ⓑ How come you can't spell apple?
"Apple" 這個字你為什麼不會拼？

📞 **舉一反三學起來！**

- Why did you flunk your spelling test?
  為什麼你的拼寫考試不及格？
- What's going on with your English quizzes this semester?
  你這學期的英語測驗怎麼搞的？

關鍵字 ▶ flunk 不及格；未通過考試、quiz 測驗、semester 學期

大師提點 🗣️ 相對而言，"how come" 比 "why" 略為不正式，不過至少好幾百年以來，這兩個字詞在語意上已經相差無幾了。

11 No vs. No can do

No 不；不是；沒有

學校 No, I'm not a doctor. I am a student.
不，我不是醫生。我是學生。

老外 **No can do**
沒辦法

實境對話 MP3 011

Ⓐ Could you help me move on Saturday?
星期六你可以幫忙我搬家嗎？

Ⓑ Sorry, no can do. I have plans this weekend.
抱歉，沒辦法。這週末我有事。

舉一反三學起來！

- I wish I could give you a hand, but I can't this weekend.
但願我可以幫你一個忙，可是這週末我沒辦法。

- I'd like to help, but this weekend isn't good for me.
我很想幫你，但這週末我不方便。

關鍵字 ▶ move 搬家、give sb. a hand 幫助某人、[time] isn't good for sb.（時間）對某人不方便

大師提點 語言學家認為 "no can do" 這個具有 200 年歷史的片語最初是對中國移民說的洋涇濱英語 (pidgin English) 的嘲諷模仿，也就是「不能做」的直譯。不過，現今那層負面涵義已然消失，並且連同它的反義詞 "can do"（可以）經常被用來回應他人的請求。

12 Take vs. Take it

 ◄◄◄ 說法比一比 ►►►

學校 **Take 拿**
Please take out your workbook. 請拿出習作本。

老外 **Take it**
受得了

🗨 實境對話　MP3 012

A I heard you quit your job.
聽說你辭職了。

B Yeah, I just couldn't take it anymore.
對啊，我真的再也受不了了。

⚡ 舉一反三學起來！

● I couldn't stand working there another month.
我受不了在那再工作一個月了。

● I tried to stick it out, but it was just too much.
我試著要撐下去，但實在是不堪負荷。

關鍵字 ▶ take out 拿出來、workbook 習作本；練習簿、stand it 承受、stick it out 堅持到底；挺住

大師提點 除了「忍受」之義外，"take it" 還能用來表示「猜想」，例如 "I take it you don't care for my cooking." 「我想你應該不喜歡我煮的菜」，以及表達「承擔某事的責任」，例如 "I'll chop the vegetables, and you take it from there." 「我來切菜，然後就交給你負責」。

13 Get vs. I got you

Get 得到

學校 I got a birthday present from my mom.
我收到了媽媽送的生日禮物。

老外 **I got you.**
我罩你。

實境對話　MP3 013

Ⓐ Oh, man. I don't think I can afford this place.
噢，天啊！這家店我吃不起。

Ⓑ Don't worry about it. I got you.
放心，我罩你。

舉一反三學起來！

● No worries. I'll take care of it.
別擔心，我會處理。

● It's cool. I've got your back.
沒事。放心，我會照應你。

關鍵字 ▸ afford 負擔得起

大師提點 你可能認為你早已經很熟 "get" 這個字，但它所形成的意思比你想像的更多。即便是 "I got you." 也至少有三個不同的涵義：「我罩你」、「哈哈！你上當了！」，還有「我明白你的意思」。Got it?

14 With vs. Down with

 ◄◄◄ **說法比一比** ►►►

學校 **With 和**
Do you want to play with me? 你想跟我一起玩嗎？

老外 **Down with**
同意；樂意去做

💬 實境對話　MP3 014

Ⓐ A bunch of us are going surfing tomorrow. Want to come?
我們一群人明天要去衝浪。想來嗎？

Ⓑ Yeah, I'm down with that.
好啊，我也要去。

舉一反三學起來！

● Sure. I'm totally up for a day at the beach.
太好了。來去海邊說定了。

● Sounds great. I'd love to.
聽起來很棒。我很樂意。

關鍵字 ➤ surfing 衝浪

大師提點 🔊 "Down with" 在這裡是俚語用法（非常口語），意思是「同意」或「雙方友好」，例如 "You're down with the volleyball team. Ask them if they want to come." 「你跟排球隊混得很熟，問他們要不要來。」而用在祈使句時，它的意思則是「打倒」，例如 "Down with the patriarchy!"「打倒父權體制！」。

27

15 Not vs. Not all there

 ◄◄◄ 說法比一比 ►►►

學校 **Not 不**
I am a student, not a teacher. 我是一名學生，不是老師。

老外 **Not all there**
精神有點錯亂／不正常

💬 實境對話　MP3 015

🅐 Sometimes I think Professor Farnsworth is not all there, if you know what I mean.
有時候我覺得方斯沃斯教授精神有點恍惚，你懂我在說什麼。

🅑 Yeah, I had a hard time following his lecture today.
對啊，今天他的課很難理解。

📞 舉一反三學起來！

- Did Professor Klump seem out of it to you?
  在你看來克倫普教授是不是有點心不在焉？
- Professor Frink wasn't quite himself today, was he?
  佛林克教授今天有點心神不寧，對吧？

關鍵字 ▶ professor 教授、have a hard time 有困難（做某事）、lecture 課程；講座、be oneself 處於正常狀態

大師提點 🗨 "Not all there" 用以委婉描述某人因年老、事故、疾病或怪癖等緣故而精神狀態不佳。另外，"not at all" 則是一種友好而禮貌的說法，指「不客氣」，兩者不宜混淆。

16 Go vs. Go-to

 ◄◄◄ 說法比一比 ►►►

Go 去；離去；行走

學校 My mom had to go to school on Saturdays.
我媽媽每週六都必須去上課。

- -

老外 **Go-to**
必去的；必找的；必做（某事）的

實境對話　MP3 016

Ⓐ What's good here?
這裡什麼好吃？

Ⓑ Sesame paste noodles and blanched greens is my go-to order at this place.
這家店的麻醬麵和燙青菜是我必點的餐點。

舉一反三學起來！

- I usually get the pork chop rice, but everything's pretty tasty.
  我通常都點豬排飯，不過每一樣餐點都滿好吃的。
- If you've never been here, you have to try the beef noodles.
  如果你是第一次來這裡，那你必須試試牛肉麵。

關鍵字 ▶ sesame paste noodles 麻醬麵、blanched greens 燙青菜、pork chop rice 豬排飯、beef noodles 牛肉麵

大師提點 說到 "to-go" 餐點（外帶／外賣），相信台灣人都相當熟悉，不過在這裡我們學到顛倒一下字序，這個字就有了全新的涵義。"Go-to" 可作形容詞 "my go-to order"「我必點的餐飲」，或名詞 "noodles are my go-to"「麵類是我的必點餐」。這個字也很常用於描述人，例如 "Jo is our go-to person for computer problems."「喬是我們解決電腦問題的首要人選」。

17 Time vs. In no time

 ◄◄◄ 說法比一比 ►►►

學校 **Time** 時間
It's time for another English quiz. 英語測驗的時間又來囉。

老外 **In no time**
很快

實境對話 MP3 017

Ⓐ Don't worry. I'll have the report done in no time.
別擔心。我很快就會把報告給完成。

Ⓑ That's what you said last week.
你上禮拜就這麼說了。

舉一反三學起來！

- I'll knock it out just like that.
  我會三兩下迅速搞定它。

- It should hardly take me any time at all.
  這根本不會花我什麼時間。

關鍵字 ▶ report 報告、knock sth. out 搞定某事、hardly 幾乎不、any time at all 很快

大師提點 去掉 "in no time" 中的 "no"，我們得到另一個至少具有三種不同涵義的常用片語。"In time" 可指「及時地」，例如 "We got here just in time."「我們正好及時來到這裡」)、也可指「最後」，例如 "Everything will be made clear in time."「最終一切都會水落石出」，以及「合節拍」的意思，例如 "If he ever learns to dance in time with the music, he'll be a star."「假如他學會隨著音樂節拍跳舞，他將是明日之星」。

18 Do vs. Do the thing

 ◀◀ 説法比一比 ▶▶

學校 **Do** 做
I do homework every day. 我每天都要做功課。

老外 **Do the thing**
就做那件事

💬 實境對話 　MP3 018

Ⓐ I'm really not looking forward to getting that root canal.
我並不期待去做那根管治療啊。

Ⓑ Yeah, I bet. But sometimes you've just got to do the thing.
嗯,我懂。不過,有時候有些事就是非做不可。

🎵 舉一反三學起來!

● What can I say? You just have to suck it up.
我能說什麼?別無選擇,做就對了。

● Just bite the bullet and get it done.
只能硬著頭皮面對,撐過去。

關鍵字 ▶ look forward to 期盼、root canal 牙齒根管治療、suck it up 忍耐;不抱怨、bite the bullet 咬緊牙關應付、get it done 完成某事

大師提點 🖐 三十多年前 Nike 創造了 "Just do it" 這個標語。而如今,老外常用 "do the thing" 來鼓勵某人做一些困難或不愉快的事情。當要激勵他人時(尤其在動作片中),通常會說:"Let's do this thing!"「我們儘管衝吧!」,有時也會縮寫成 "Let's do this!",表示「我們放手一搏吧!」。

19 Good vs. Good for

 ◀◀◀ 說法比一比 ▶▶▶

學校 **Good** 好的
You did a good job! 你做得很好！

老外 **Good for**
有支付……能力的

實境對話 MP3 019

A You want me to lend you five hundred dollars for lunch?
你要我借你五百元買午餐？

B Yeah. C'mon! I'm good for it.
嗯，拜託！我有錢能還你。

舉一反三學起來！

- I'll pay you back.
  我會還你。
- I'll get it next time.
  下次我請客。

關鍵字 ▶ pay sb. back 還錢給某人、get it 買單

大師提點 當有人說他們 "good for (the money)" 時，意思是指他們肯定會還你的。"Good for" 也用於讚美，例如 "Good for you!"「真棒！」、用於「建議」，例如 "Honey is good for a sore throat."「吃點蜂蜜能緩解喉嚨痛」，以及談論某樣東西能用多久，例如 "The yogurt in the fridge is good for another week."，表示「冰箱裡的優格還能再吃一個禮拜」。

20 From vs. From the get-go

 ◄◄◄ 說法比一比 ►►►

學校 **From 從**
My grandfather is from Hualien. 我的祖父是花蓮人。

老外 **From the get-go**
從一開始

🗨 實境對話　MP3 020

A What could we have done differently?
我們本可以做些什麼不同的事？

B Nothing. The project was doomed from the get-go.
沒有。這個案子從一開始就註定會失敗。

🖊 舉一反三學起來！

- We started having problems right from the very beginning.
打從一開始我們就面臨了一些困難。

- I knew we were in trouble from the time the project was announced.
打從這個專案宣布開始，我就知道我們遇到了麻煩。

關鍵字 ▶ doomed 註定失敗 / 滅亡的

大師提點 🗨 沒有人確定 "from the get-go" 是從何時開始意味著某事的開端，但它可能與 "get going" 有關。不意外地，許多與「開始」相關的時間說法都以 "from" 開頭，例如同樣是「從一開始」意思的 "from the word go"，以及同樣表達「從現在開始」的 "from now on" 和 "from here on (out)"。

Warmed up? Good!
Let's get started.

口語必通篇

Part 1
基本對話必備

1 表達感謝

 ◄◄◄ 說法比一比 ►►►

學校 **Thank you.**
謝謝。

老外 **Thank you so much. I really appreciate all your help.**
非常謝謝你。我十分感激你幫的所有忙。

💬 實境對話 MP3 021

Ⓐ Well, the surgery was successful. She's going to be just fine.
嗯，手術很成功，她會好起來的。

Ⓑ Thank you so much, doctor. I really appreciate all your help.
非常謝謝您，醫生。我十分感激您幫的所有忙。

🎵 舉一反三學起來！

● I really want to thank you.
我真的想要感謝你。

● I really appreciate what you said.
我十分感激你說的話。

● I really appreciate everything you've done for us.
我十分感激你為我們所做的一切。

關鍵字 ➤ appreciate 感激

大師提點 🗣 "Thank you." 當然是正確英文。但有時候，你需要為你的感謝添加一點色彩，那上述所建議的替代說法就能派上用場了。

2 回應感謝

 ◀◀◀ 說法比一比 ▶▶▶

學校 **You're welcome.**
不客氣。

老外 **No problem.**
哪裡。

💬 實境對話 MP3 022

Ⓐ Thanks for the coffee.
咖啡謝了。

Ⓑ No problem.
哪裡。

✍ 舉一反三學起來！

● Sure. Any time.
沒什麼，有需要隨時開口。

● Don't mention it.
別放在心上。

● Not a big deal.
沒什麼。

關鍵字 ➤ mention 提及、a big deal 大事情

大師提點 🗣 使用 "You're welcome." 不會出錯，這是比較正式的說法，但當你的對象是朋友，或者你幫別人的忙不是特別偉大時，不妨使用比較沒那麼正式的回答。

3 為小事道歉

 ◀◀◀ 說法比一比 ▶▶▶

學校 **I'm sorry.**
對不起。

老外 **Sorry about that!**
不好意思！

💬 實境對話　MP3 023

Ⓐ Hey, what are you doing?
嘿，你在做什麼？

Ⓑ Sorry about that!
不好意思！

🎵 舉一反三學起來！

- Sorry, I didn't mean to do that.
  抱歉，我不是有意這麼做的。
- Sorry, I shouldn't have done that.
  抱歉，我不該這麼做的。
- I'm sorry. That was my fault.
  我很抱歉。那是我的錯。

大師提點 🎤 道歉的語調應視所出的紕漏有多嚴重而定。最好能準備多種可能的回答，「舉一反三學起來！」的句子還加上了簡短的解釋或坦承。

◄◄◄ 說法比一比 ►►►

學校 **I'm sorry.**
我很抱歉。

老外 **I'm so sorry. How can I make it up to you?**
我非常抱歉。我可以怎麼補償你？

實境對話 MP3 024

Ⓐ I've had that car for less than a month. Look what you've done to it!
我買那輛車還不到一個月。看你把它弄成什麼樣子？

Ⓑ Oh my God. I'm so sorry. How can I make it up to you?
我的天哪。我非常抱歉。我可以怎麼補償你？

舉一反三學起來！

● I can't tell you how sorry I am. It won't happen again.
我無法形容我有多抱歉。下不為例。

● Please accept my apologies. I'll do whatever it takes to make it up to you.
請接受我的道歉。我會盡全力補償你。

關鍵字 ► make it up 補償、accept one's apology 接受某人的道歉

5 接受道歉

 ◀◀◀ 說法比一比 ▶▶▶

[Sorry about that!]

學校 That's fine.
沒關係。

[Sorry about that!]

老外 That's OK.
沒關係。

💬 實境對話 MP3 025

Ⓐ Sorry about that!
那件事很抱歉！

Ⓑ That's OK.
沒關係。

☎ 舉一反三學起來！

- Don't worry about it.
  別放在心上。
- It's not a big deal.
  沒什麼。
- Forget it.
  算了。

關鍵字 ▶ worry 擔心、forget 忘記

6 請求協助

學校 **I need your help.**
我需要你幫忙。

老外 **I could really use your help.**
我真的需要你的幫忙。

💬 實境對話 MP3 026

Ⓐ You look exhausted. Anything I can do?
你看起來累翻了。有什麼我可以做的嗎？

Ⓑ Yeah, I could really use your help.
有，我真的需要你的幫忙。

舉一反三學起來！

- I could really use a hand.
  我真的需要人幫忙。
- I'd really appreciate a little help with this.
  要是能得到一點協助，我會十分感激。

關鍵字 ➤ use one's help 需要某人幫忙、use a hand 需要幫忙

大師提點 🗣 "I could use your help." 是比 "I need your help." 委婉、客氣的請求。

7 示意欲結束談話

 ◀◀◀ **說法比一比** ▶▶▶

學校 **I have to leave now.**
我現在得走了。

老外 **I should be going soon.**
我馬上就該走了。

💬 **實境對話** MP3 027

Ⓐ I should be going soon.
我馬上就該走了。

Ⓑ Oh, OK. Well, let's get together again sometime.
喔,好。那改天再聚吧。

🎯 **舉一反三學起來!**

● I should be getting back.
我該回去了。

● I've got to head out in a little while.
我馬上就得閃人了。

關鍵字 ▶ get together 聚在一起、head out 離開

大師提點 🗨 用 "I have to leave now." 來結束談話稍嫌直接,須依談話的對象謹慎使用。

8 道別

學校 **Bye-bye.**
掰掰。

老外 **Good-bye.**
再見。

實境對話 MP3 028

🅐 Good-bye and good luck with your new job.
再見,祝你新工作順利。

🅑 OK. Thank you Professor Chen. Good-bye.
好的,謝謝陳教授。再見。

舉一反三學起來!

- It was good to see you.
  很高興跟你見面。
- Take care.
  保重。
- Keep in touch.
  保持聯絡。
- See you later.
  回頭見。

大師提點 🗣 "Bye-bye." 通常沒什麼問題,但有時候聽起來太俏皮了,好像是在跟小孩道別一樣。"Good-bye." 則是比較正式的用法,通常表示有一段時間不會再見面。

44

9 撥打電話

 ◀◀◀ 說法比一比 ▶▶▶

學校 **May I talk to Mr. Chuang?**
我可以跟莊先生講話嗎？

老外 **May I speak with Mr. Chuang, please?**
麻煩可以找莊先生講話嗎？

實境對話 MP3 029

Ⓐ Hello. May I speak with Mr. Chuang, please?
喂，麻煩可以找莊先生講話嗎？

Ⓑ May I ask who's calling?
請問哪裡找？

舉一反三學起來！

● Is Mr. Chuang available?
莊先生在嗎？

● Is Mr. Chuang there?
莊先生在那裡嗎？

關鍵字 ▶ speak with sb. 和某人講話、available 有空

10 轉接電話

學校 **I'll transfer the call for you.**
我幫您把電話轉過去。

老外 **I'll transfer you.**
我為您轉接。

💬 實境對話　MP3 030

A Hi, I'm trying to reach Mike Pan.
嗨，我要找麥克‧潘。

B Just a moment please. I'll transfer you.
請等一下。我為您轉接。

🎧 舉一反三學起來！

- I'll transfer your call.
  我把您的電話轉過去。
- I'm transferring you now.
  我現在幫您轉接。
- Please hold. I'll put you through.
  請稍候。我幫您轉過去。

關鍵字 ▸ transfer 轉接、hold 等一下、put sb. through 幫某人轉接

46

11 打錯電話

 ◄◄◄ 說法比一比 ►►►

學校 **I'm not sure whether we have that person.**
我不確定我們有沒有這個人。

老外 **There's no one here by that name.**
這裡沒有叫這名字的人。

💬 實境對話　MP3 031

Ⓐ Is Ms. Yu there?
于小姐在嗎？

Ⓑ I'm sorry, there's no one here by that name.
抱歉，這裡沒有叫這名字的人。

🎵 舉一反三學起來！

- I think you have the wrong number.
  我想你打錯電話了。

關鍵字 ▶ no one by that name 沒有叫這名字的人、have the wrong number 打錯號碼

47

12 詢問時間

 ◄◄◄ **說法比一比** ►►►

學校 **What time is it now?**
現在幾點了？

老外 **Do you have the time?**
你知道幾點了嗎？

實境對話　MP3 032

Ⓐ Excuse me. Do you have the time?
請問一下，你知道幾點了嗎？

Ⓑ Yeah, it's 10:15.
知道，十點十五分。

舉一反三學起來！

● Do you know what time it is?
你知道現在幾點了嗎？

● What time do you have?
你知不知道幾點了？

關鍵字 ▶ have the time 知道時間

大師提點 另外，要詢問日期的說法為 "What's the date today?"；詢問星期幾則為 "What day is it today?"。Date 指的是日期；day 則指星期幾。

Part 2

邀約

What will you do this weekend?
VS
What are you doing this weekend?

1 詢問是否有計畫

 ◄◄◄ **說法比一比** ►►►

學校 **What will you do this weekend?**
你這個週末要做什麼？

老外 **What are you doing this weekend?**
你這個週末要做什麼？

實境對話　MP3 033

Ⓐ What are you doing this weekend?
你這個週末要做什麼？

Ⓑ I don't know yet.
我還不曉得。

舉一反三學起來！

● What are your plans for the weekend?
你這個週末有什麼計畫？
● Do you have any plans for the weekend?
你這個週末有任何計畫嗎？

關鍵字 ▶ weekend 週末、plan 計畫

大師提點 老外常用「進行式」來詢問未來計畫，而非 will。

2 詢問是否有空

 ◄◄◄ **說法比一比** ►►►

學校 **Do you have free time tomorrow?**
你明天有空嗎？

老外 **Do you have time tomorrow?**
你明天有空嗎？

實境對話 　MP3 034

Ⓐ Do you have time tomorrow?
你明天有空嗎？
Ⓑ What do you have in mind?
你有什麼想法？

舉一反三學起來！

● Are you doing anything tomorrow?
你明天有要做什麼嗎？
● When are you free?
你什麼時候有空？
● When's good for you?
你什麼時候可以？
● When can we get together?
我們什麼時候可以聚一聚？
● When would be a good time?
什麼時候比較方便？

關鍵字 ▸ free 有空

3 表示有空

 ◀◀◀ **說法比一比** ▶▶▶

[When should we meet?]

學校 **I'm free every day.**
我每天都有空。

[When should we meet?]

老外 **Anytime is good with me.**
我隨時都可以。

💬 實境對話　MP3 035

A When should we meet?
我們該什麼時候見面？

B Anytime is good with me.
我隨時都可以。

👂 舉一反三學起來！

● I'm usually free in the evenings.
我通常晚上都有空。

● Weekday afternoons are usually good for me.
平日下午我通常都可以。

● Any day except Thursday works for me.
除了星期四，我哪一天都行。

關鍵字 ▶ good 合適、work for me 對我來說行得通

52

4 表示沒空

 ◄◄◄ 說法比一比 ►►►

[Let's have dinner one night this week.]

學校 **I'm sorry. I'm too busy.**
抱歉。我太忙了。

[Let's have dinner one night this week.]

老外 **I'm sorry. This is a really busy time for me.**
抱歉。這段時間我忙得不得了。

實境對話   MP3 036

A Let's have dinner one night this week.
這星期找一天晚上吃晚餐吧。

B I'm sorry. This is a really busy time for me.
抱歉。這段時間我忙得不得了。

舉一反三學起來！

- I'm busy all week.
  我整個星期都很忙。
- Next week would be better for me.
  下星期對我來說比較好。
- I'm not sure when I'm going to have time.
  我不確定我什麼時候會有空。

關鍵字 ▸ busy 忙碌

5 對邀約不置可否

 ◄◄◄ **說法比一比** ►►►

[What are you doing this weekend?]

學校 **I don't know.**
我不曉得耶。

[What are you doing this weekend?]

老外 **I may see a friend. I'm not sure yet.**
我也許會和朋友見面。我還不確定。

🗨 實境對話　MP3 037

Ⓐ What are you doing this weekend?
你這個週末要做什麼？

Ⓑ I may see a friend. I'm not sure yet.
我也許會和朋友見面。我還不確定。

🎵 舉一反三學起來！

- I haven't really thought about it.
  我還沒有認真想過。
- I'm still trying to figure that out.
  我還在努力思考。
- That depends on a lot of things.
  那要視許多因素而定。

關鍵字 ► figure out 想出；理解、depend on 視……而定

54

6 | 婉拒邀約

 ◄◄◄ 說法比一比 ►►►

[Want to get a beer after work?]

學校 **No, thank you.**
不了，謝謝。

[Want to get a beer after work?]

老外 **I wish I could. Maybe another time.**
但願可以。也許改天吧。

🗨 實境對話　MP3 038

A Want to get a beer after work?
下班後想喝個啤酒嗎？

B I wish I could. Maybe another time.
但願可以。也許改天吧。

🎵 舉一反三學起來！

- Not tonight. I can't.
  今天晚上我不行。
- I already have plans tonight.
  我今天晚上已經有計畫了。
- I'm not really a beer person.
  我不是很愛喝啤酒的人。

大師提點 🗨 "No, thank you." 帶有斷然拒絕的意味。假如你想傳達的就是這種印象（例如回應不想要的邀約），那就儘管用吧。但通常會用像是 "I wish I could ..." 此肯定句法來表達委婉的拒絕。

◀◀◀ **説法比一比** ▶▶▶

[Want to get a beer after work?]

學校 **Yes, I do.**
好，我去。

[Want to get a beer after work?]

老外 **Sounds good.**
聽起來不錯。

實境對話 MP3 039

Ⓐ Want to get a beer after work?
下班後想喝個啤酒嗎？

Ⓑ Sounds good.
聽起來不錯。

舉一反三學起來！

- Sure, that would be great.
  沒問題，那太好了。
- Yeah, I'd love to.
  好啊，樂意之至。

關鍵字 ▶ sound 聽起來……

8 說明地點

 ◀◀◀ 說法比一比 ▶▶▶

學校 **It's at the crossroads of Hoping and Jinshan.**
它在和平與金山的交叉口。

老外 **It's near Hoping and Jinshan.**
它在和平與金山附近。

💬 實境對話 MP3 040

A Where's the restaurant?
餐廳在哪裡？

B It's near Hoping and Jinshan.
在和平與金山附近。

🔔 舉一反三學起來！

- The cross streets are Hoping and Jinshan.
交叉的街道是和平與金山。
- It's at the intersection of Hoping and Jinshan.
在和平與金山的交叉處。
- It's right on the corner of Hoping and Jinshan.
就在和平與金山路口。

關鍵字 ▶ intersection 交叉口、on the corner 在街角

大師提點 🗣 老外在說明地點時很少用 crossroad 這個字，而會直接用 near 來說明地點靠近何處。

9 指示方向

 ◄◄◄ **説法比一比** ►►►

學校 **When you go out of the MRT station, turn right.**
等你出了捷運站就往右轉。

老外 **When you get out of the station, turn right.**
你出了車站就右轉。

🗨 實境對話　MP3 041

Ⓐ Hi, I just got off the train. Where do I go?
嗨，我剛下車。我該怎麼走？

Ⓑ OK. When you get out of the station, turn right.
好，你出了車站就右轉。

🎵 舉一反三學起來！

- After you come out of the station, turn right.
  你走出車站後就右轉。
- As soon as you come out of the station, turn right.
  你一走出車站就右轉。

關鍵字 ▶ turn 轉彎

大師提點 🗣 Turn right 常被誤用為 go right，讀者要留意！

10 確認 / 提醒

 ◄◄◄ **說法比一比** ►►►

學校 **I want to confirm our date for Friday.**
我想確認一下我們星期五的約會。

老外 **We're still on for Friday night, right?**
我們還是約星期五晚上，對吧？

🗨 實境對話　MP3 042

Ⓐ We're still on for Friday night, right?
我們還是約星期五晚上，對吧？
Ⓑ Yeah.
是啊。

🔑 舉一反三學起來！

● See you on Friday, right?
星期五見，對吧？
● Don't forget our dinner on Friday, OK?
別忘了星期五的晚餐，好嗎？

關鍵字 ▶ still on 還是成立（此處指我們還是約定某時間，後接 for 來說明時間。）

11 取消

 ◄◄◄ 說法比一比 ►►►

學校 **I can't go.**
我不能去。

老外 **I'm not going to be able to make it.**
我去不了了。

💬 實境對話　MP3 043

Ⓐ See you on Friday, right?
星期五見，對吧？

Ⓑ Actually, I'm not going to be able to make it.
其實我去不了了。

🎵 舉一反三學起來！

- I'm afraid I'm going to have to reschedule our dinner.
  我恐怕必須把晚餐改期了。
- I was going to ask you if we could make it for another time.
  我本打算要問你，我們能不能改天再約。

關鍵字 ➤ make it 辦得到；去得成、reschedule 改期

12 遲到

 ◄◄◄ **說法比一比** ►►►

學校 **Sorry, I'm late.**
抱歉，我遲到了。

老外 **Sorry I kept you waiting.**
抱歉讓你等我。

💬 實境對話　MP3 044

A What took you?
你怎麼了？

B Sorry I kept you waiting. I had a little trouble finding the place.
抱歉讓你等我。我有點找不到地方。

🔑 舉一反三學起來！

● I got a late start.
我出發晚了。
● Traffic was terrible.
塞車很嚴重。

Ch 1

Part 2

邀約

關鍵字 ► have trouble + Ving（做……有困難）、late start 延遲出發

1 問候 1

學校 **How are you?**
你好嗎？

老外 **How are you doing?**
近來好嗎？

實境對話 MP3 045

A Hey, how are you doing?
嘿，近來好嗎？

B I'm doing OK, and you?
不錯啊。你呢？

舉一反三學起來！

- How's it going?
  還好嗎？
- How's everything?
  一切可好？
- How have you been?
  你近來怎麼樣？

2 問候 2

  ◄◄◄ 說法比一比 ►►►

學校 **What are you doing recently?**
你最近在做些什麼？

老外 **What have you been up to?**
你都在忙什麼？

🗨️ **實境對話** MP3 046

Ⓐ What have you been up to?
你都在忙什麼？

Ⓑ Not too much.
沒什麼。

🎷 **舉一反三學起來！**

- What's new with you?
  你有什麼新鮮事嗎？
- What's new?
  有什麼新鮮事嗎？
- What's up?
  過得怎麼樣？

關鍵字 ▶ be up to 正從事於；忙於

3 回應問候 1

 ◄◄◄ 說法比一比 ►►►

[How are you doing?]

學校 I'm fine, thank you. And you?
我很好,謝謝。你呢?

[How are you doing?]

老外 Not bad. And yourself?
還不錯。你自己呢?

💬 實境對話 MP3 047

A How are you doing?
你好嗎?

B Not bad. And yourself?
還不錯。你自己呢?

🔑 舉一反三學起來!

- Not so good.
  不太好。
- Could be worse.
  不算太糟。
- Can't complain.
  沒什麼可抱怨的。
- Pretty good.
  好得很。
- Everything's great.
  一切都很好。

4 回應問候 2

 ◀◀◀ 說法比一比 ▶▶▶

[What's new?]

學校 **I'm fine. Just as usual.**
我很好。就跟平常一樣。

[What's new?]

老外 **Not much. Busy as usual.**
沒什麼。跟平常一樣忙。

實境對話 MP3 048

Ⓐ What's new?
有什麼新鮮事？

Ⓑ Not much. Busy as usual.
沒什麼。跟平常一樣忙。

舉一反三學起來！

● Same old.
老樣子。

● I'm keeping busy.
我一直很忙。

關鍵字 ▸ as usual 跟平常一樣

66

5 歡迎對方

 ◄◄◄ 說法比一比 ►►►

學校 **You're here!**
你來了！

老外 **You made it!**
你到了！

 **MP3 049**

A You made it!
你到了！
B Yeah, it took me forever to find this place.
是啊，我找了超久才找到這個地方。

🖋 舉一反三學起來！

- It's good to see you.
  見到你真好。
- I'm so glad you could come.
  真高興你能來。
- I wasn't sure you were coming.
  我都不確定你會來。

6 初次見面

 ◄◄◄ 說法比一比 ►►►

學校 **How do you do?**
你好嗎？

老外 **Nice to meet you.**
幸會。

💬 實境對話 　MP3 050

Ⓐ This is my boss, Ms. Yan.
這是我老闆顏小姐。

Ⓑ Nice to meet you.
幸會。

✍ 舉一反三學起來！

● Nice meeting you.
幸會。

● Ms. Yan.
顏小姐。
（如上述對話情境，如果有第三方先介紹彼此，則可用對方的名字來打招呼。）

大師提點 🗨 "How do you do?" 是正確用法，只不過在大部分的場合中都太正式了。

7 詢問電話號碼

  ◀◀◀ 說法比一比 ▶▶▶

學校 **May I have your telephone number?**
我可以要你的電話號碼嗎？

老外 **Could I get your number?**
我可不可以要你的號碼？

實境對話　MP3 051

A Could I get your number?
我可不可以要你的號碼？
B Sure.
當然可以。

舉一反三學起來！

- Could you give me your cell number?
  可以給我你的手機號碼嗎？
- What's your number?
  你的電話是多少？
- What's your cell number?
  你的手機號碼是多少？

關鍵字 ▶ number（電話）號碼、cell number 手機號碼

Part 4
表達感受

1 遺憾

 ◀◀◀ 說法比一比 ▶▶▶

學校 **It's a pity.**
那真可惜。

老外 **That's too bad.**
那太糟了。

實境對話　MP3 052

Ⓐ My boyfriend just got fired.
我男朋友剛被解雇了。

Ⓑ That's too bad.
那太糟了。

舉一反三學起來！

● That's awful.
那真糟糕。
● I'm sorry to hear that.
我很遺憾聽到這件事。

關鍵字 ▶ awful 糟糕的

大師提點 學校還教了 "It's a pity that + 子句" 的用法，但通常老外只會針對事情直接了當地回應 "That's too bad."。

71

2 期望

學校 **My professor hopes I can finish the paper by Friday.**
我的教授希望我能在星期五前把論文寫完。

老外 **My professor asked me to finish the paper by Friday.**
我的教授要我在星期五前把論文寫完。

實境對話　MP3 053

Ⓐ My professor asked me to finish the paper by Friday.
我的教授要我在星期五前把論文寫完。

Ⓑ I hope you weren't planning on doing anything else this week.
希望你這個星期沒打算做什麼其他的事。

舉一反三學起來！

● My boss is making us work overtime this week.
老闆要我們這星期加班。

● My parents want us to come over for dinner on Sunday.
我爸媽要我們星期天去吃晚飯。

關鍵字 ▶ finish 完成、work overtime 加班

大師提點 在表示期望時，老外不見得會用 hope 這個字，反而較常使用 ask、make、want 等較直接的字眼。

3 關心

 ◄◄◄ **說法比一比** ►►►

學校 **I hope you recover soon.**
希望你早日康復。

老外 **Get well soon.**
早日康復。

💬 實境對話　[MP3] 054

Ⓐ Could you tell Mr. Chu that I've got a cold and won't come in today?
你能不能告訴朱先生我感冒了，今天不進去了？

Ⓑ Sure. Get well soon.
沒問題。早日康復。

🖊 舉一反三學起來！

- Are you OK?
  你還好嗎？
- Is there anything you need?
  你有沒有需要什麼？
- Take care of yourself.
  好好保重。

關鍵字 ▶ get well 康復、take care of 照顧

4 後悔懊惱

學校 **I regret that I chose architecture as my major.**
我真後悔選了建築作為主修。

老外 **I shouldn't have chosen architecture as my major.**
我不該選建築作為主修的。

💬 實境對話 MP3 055

A I shouldn't have chosen architecture as my major.
我不該選建築作為主修的。

B Well, there's nothing you can do about that now.
嗯，現在你也無能為力了。

🎵 舉一反三學起來！

- I shouldn't have done that.
  我不該這麼做的。
- I really messed up.
  我真的搞砸了。
- I really blew it.
  我真的搞砸了。

關鍵字 ▶ mess up 搞砸、blow 搞砸

5 悲傷難過

 ◀◀◀ 說法比一比 ▶▶▶

學校 **I'm sad.**
我很悲傷。

老外 **I'm feeling a little down.**
我心情有點不好。

實境對話　MP3 056

Ⓐ Are you OK?
你還好嗎？

Ⓑ I'm feeling a little down.
我心情有點不好。

舉一反三學起來！

● I guess I'm not in a very good mood.
我想我心情不是很好。

● I'm absolutely miserable.
我真是慘斃了。

關鍵字 ▶ down 心情低落、mood 情緒、miserable 可憐的

75

6 加油打氣

 ◀◀◀ **說法比一比** ▶▶▶

學校 **Cheer up!**
開心一點！

- -

老外 **It'll be OK.**
會沒事的。

實境對話　MP3 057

A　I can't believe I didn't get the job.
　　我不敢相信我沒得到那份工作。
B　It'll be OK.
　　會沒事的。

舉一反三學起來！

- It just takes a little time.
  只是需要一點時間。
- Hang in there.
  撐下去。

大師提點 "Cheer up!" 是在此情境的典型說法，導致失了一點誠懇度。如果想讓對方真正感到窩心，試試別的說法吧！

Chapter 2

聊天有梗篇

Part 1

關於個人

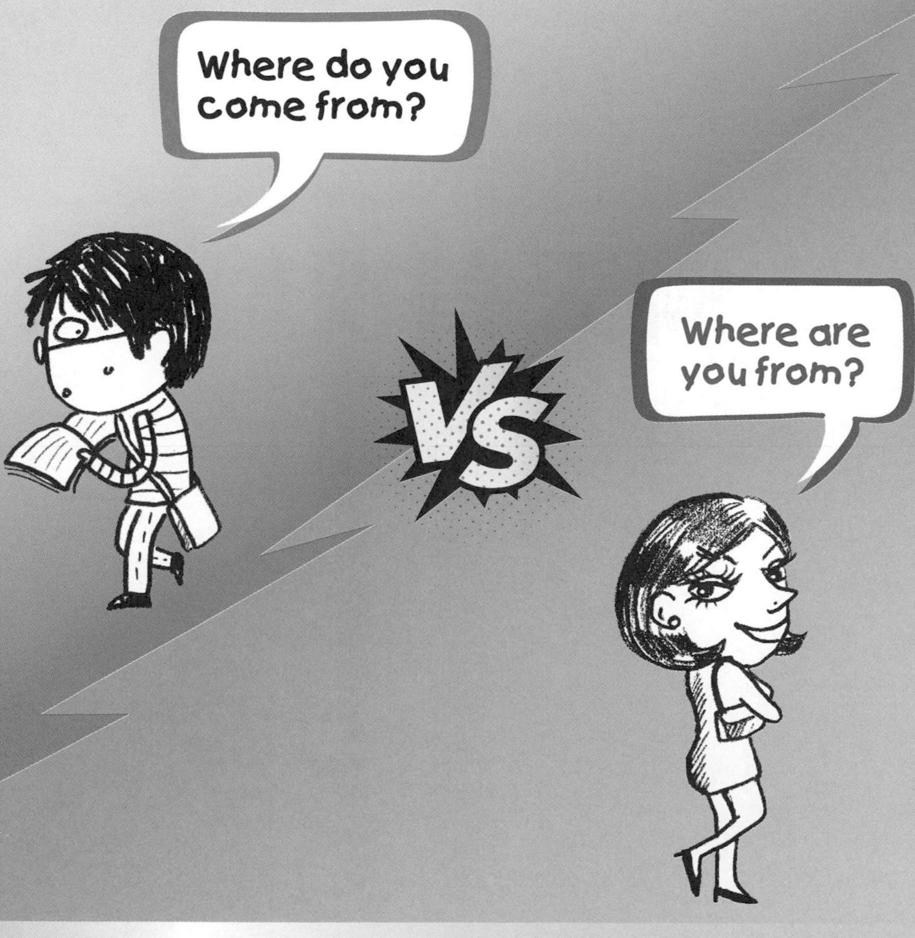

1 詢問對方哪裡人

 ◀◀◀ **說法比一比** ▶▶▶

學校 **Where do you come from?**
你從哪裡來的？

老外 **Where are you from?**
你來自哪裡？

💬 實境對話 　MP3 058

A Actually, English isn't my first language.
其實英語不是我的母語。

B I didn't know that. Where are you from?
我不曉得這件事。你來自哪裡？

🎵 舉一反三學起來！

● Where's home?
老家在哪裡？
● Where did you grow up?
你在哪裡長大的？
● Are you from around here?
你來自這附近嗎？
● Are you from New York originally?
你原本就是紐約人嗎？

關鍵字 ▶ from 來自、originally 原本

2 請對方自我介紹

 ◄◄◄ **說法比一比** ►►►

學校 **Could you introduce yourself?**
你能介紹一下自己嗎？

老外 **Could you tell me about yourself?**
你能跟我談談你自己嗎？

💬 實境對話　MP3 059

Ⓐ Could you tell me about yourself?
你能跟我談談你自己嗎？

Ⓑ OK. What do you want to know?
好。你想知道什麼？

🎵 舉一反三學起來！

● How would you describe yourself?
你會怎麼形容自己？

● It seems like you're pretty laid-back.
你看起來相當隨性自在。

關鍵字 ▶ describe 描述、laid-back 從容不迫的

3 形容自己

 ◂◂◂ 說法比一比 ▸▸▸

學校 **I'm a sunny girl.**
我是個陽光女孩。

老外 **I'm a pretty positive person.**
我是個相當樂觀的人。

實境對話　MP3 060

Ⓐ I'm a pretty positive person.
我是個相當樂觀的人。
Ⓑ Yeah, I can tell.
是啊，我看得出來。

舉一反三學起來！

- I try to keep a positive attitude.
  我盡量保持正面的態度。
- I'm usually pretty optimistic.
  我通常相當樂觀。

關鍵字 ▸ positive 樂觀的；積極的、optimistic 樂觀的

4 詢問對方的計畫

 ◀◀◀ 說法比一比 ▶▶▶

學校 **What is your plan for the future?**
你對未來有什麼計畫？

老外 **Do you have any plans?**
你有任何的計畫嗎？

實境對話　MP3 061

Ⓐ I'm going to quit my job after I get my annual bonus.
等拿到了年終獎金，我就要把工作辭掉。

Ⓑ Good for you. Do you have any plans?
不錯啊。你有任何的計畫嗎？

舉一反三學起來！

● What's next?
接下來呢？

● Do you have something lined up?
你接下來有什麼安排嗎？

長期計畫

● What do you think you'll be doing this time next year?
你覺得到了明年此時，你會在做什麼？

● Where do you see yourself five years from now?
你認為五年後，你會在什麼地方？

關鍵字 ➤ something lined up 接下來的安排

Part 2
台灣

Is it your first time to come to Taiwan?

Is this your first time in Taiwan?

◀◀◀ **説法比一比** ▶▶▶

學校 **Is it your first time to come to Taiwan?**
你第一次來台灣嗎？

老外 **Is this your first time in Taiwan?**
這是你第一次到台灣嗎？

實境對話 MP3 062

Ⓐ Is this your first time in Taiwan?
這是你第一次到台灣嗎？

Ⓑ Yeah, so far everything has been great.
是啊，到目前為止一切都很不錯。

舉一反三學起來！

● Have you been to Taiwan before?
你以前去過台灣嗎？

● You've been here before, haven't you?
你以前來過這裡，對吧？

關鍵字 ▶ have been to ＋ 地方（去過……）

2 詢問對方來訪的目的

 ◄◄◄ **說法比一比** ►►►

學校 **Why did you come to Taiwan?**
你為什麼來台灣？

老外 **Are you here on business?**
你來這裡出差嗎？

🗨 實境對話 ┃ MP3 063

Ⓐ Are you here on business?
你來這裡出差嗎？

Ⓑ Yeah, I've got meetings with clients scheduled all week.
是啊，我整個星期都排定了去拜會客戶。

🎵 舉一反三學起來！

- Have you seen much of the city?
  你有在市內多看看嗎？
- Have you had a chance to get out of Taipei yet?
  你有機會去過台北以外的地方了嗎？

關鍵字 ▶ on business 出差、see the city 參觀這個城市

3 詢問對方在台灣的旅遊計畫

 ◄◄◄ 說法比一比 ►►►

學校 **What will you do in Taiwan?**
你在台灣要做什麼？

老外 **Do you have any plans while you're here?**
你在這裡的期間，有沒有什麼計畫？

實境對話　MP3 064

A Do you have any plans while you're here?
你在這裡的期間，有沒有什麼計畫？

B Not yet. I'm just playing it by ear.
還沒有。我打算見機行事。

舉一反三學起來！

● Is there anything in particular you'd like to do or see while you're here?
你在這裡的期間，有沒有特別想做或想看什麼？

● Let me know if you'd like any restaurant suggestions.
假如你想要什麼餐廳方面的建議，就跟我說一聲。

● If you'd like, I could show you around Taipei.
假如你願意的話，我可以帶你逛逛台北。

關鍵字 ▶ play by ear 見機行事；看著辦、show you around 帶你到處看看

4 詢問對方對台灣的印象

 ◀◀◀ **說法比一比** ▶▶▶

學校 **Do you like Taiwan?**
你喜歡台灣嗎？

老外 **How's your trip been so far?**
到目前為止，你的旅程怎麼樣？

💬 實境對話　MP3 065

A How's your trip been so far?
到目前為止，你的旅程怎麼樣？

B Great. Everyone here is so friendly.
很棒。這裡的每個人都十分友善。

✍ 舉一反三學起來！

- Do you have any first impressions of Taiwan?
你對台灣有什麼第一印象嗎？
- I've heard people say that Taiwan can be a little boring for short-term visitors.
我聽說，台灣對短期遊客而言會有點無聊。
- Have you seen anything interesting yet?
你參觀過什麼有趣的東西了嗎？

關鍵字 ▶ first impression 第一印象、short-term 短期的

Part 3
語言能力

Can you speak Chinese?

VS

Do you speak Chinese?

1 語言能力——中文

 ◀◀◀ 說法比一比 ▶▶▶

學校 **Can you speak Chinese?**
你會不會說中文？

老外 **Do you speak Chinese?**
你會說中文嗎？

💬 實境對話　　MP3 066

Ⓐ Do you speak Chinese?
你會說中文嗎？
Ⓑ Yeah, a little.
會，一點點。

🖊 舉一反三學起來！

● Do you know any Chinese?
你懂中文嗎？
● How's your Taiwanese?
你的台語怎麼樣？
● Do you mind if we speak Chinese?
你介意我們說中文嗎？

關鍵字 ▶ Chinese 中文、Taiwanese 台語

2 語言能力——稱讚

 ◄◄◄ 說法比一比 ►►►

學校 **Your Chinese is very good!**
你的中文非常好！

老外 **I like the way you speak Chinese.**
我喜歡你說的中文。

💬 實境對話　MP3 067

A I like the way you speak Chinese.
我喜歡你說的中文。

B That's very nice of you to say.
你真是過獎了。

🎣 舉一反三學起來！

- Your pronunciation is very natural.
  你的發音非常自然。
- I like your handwriting.
  我喜歡你的字跡。
- You've got a pretty big Chinese vocabulary.
  你懂的中文字彙相當多。

大師提點 🗨 "Your Chinese is very good!" 是正確的英文，但在台灣卻被濫用得一塌糊塗而變得毫無意義。假如是隨口評論，那無所謂。要是你真的想稱讚別人的能力，那就要使用上述比較具體的說法。

3 語言能力——自謙 1

  ◄◄◄ **說法比一比** ►►►

學校 I'm sorry. My English is very poor.
抱歉，我的英文很爛。

老外 Please let me know if you don't understand something I say.
假如你聽不懂我說的話，請告訴我一聲。

實境對話 MP3 068

Ⓐ Please let me know if you don't understand something I say.
假如你聽不懂我說的話，請告訴我一聲。

Ⓑ OK.
好。

舉一反三學起來！

● Do you know what I mean?
你明白我的意思嗎？

● Does what I'm saying make sense to you?
你聽得懂我在說什麼嗎？

● Are you following me?
你了解我的意思嗎？

關鍵字 ➤ make sense 有道理、follow 懂；理解

大師提點 ☞ "My English is very poor." 是台灣人說英文時常用的開場白，其實並非好的表達方式，英文不好，不必道歉，不必說明，只要能與聽者溝通即可。

4 語言能力──自謙 2

 ◄◄◄ **說法比一比** ►►►

學校 **I can't speak out what I want to say.**
我表達不出我想說的話。

老外 **It's hard sometimes to say exactly what I mean.**
要確切說出我的意思有時候很困難。

🗨 實境對話　MP3 069

Ⓐ It's hard sometimes to say exactly what I mean.
要確切說出我的意思有時候很困難。
Ⓑ I know exactly how you feel.
我完全明白你的感受。

§ 舉一反三學起來！

● I can't always get my point across.
我老是辭不達意。
● It's frustrating when you can't express yourself.
有話講不出來真令人洩氣。

關鍵字 ▶ get across 使了解、express 表達

5 談論學習狀況

 ◀◀ 說法比一比 ▶▶

學校 **I have few chances to speak English to foreigners.**
我沒什麼機會跟外國人說英語。

老外 **I don't have many opportunities to speak English.**
我說英語的機會不多。

🗨️ 實境對話   MP3 070

Ⓐ I don't have many opportunities to speak English.
我說英語的機會不多。

Ⓑ Really? It seems like almost everyone I've met here can speak it.
真的嗎？我在這裡遇到的人看起來幾乎個個都會說。

舉一反三學起來！

- I think my English is a little rusty.
  我想我的英文有點荒廢了。
- I spend more time reading English than speaking it.
  我讀英文的時間比說的時間多。

關鍵字 ▶ rusty 荒廢的；生疏的

Part 4

天氣

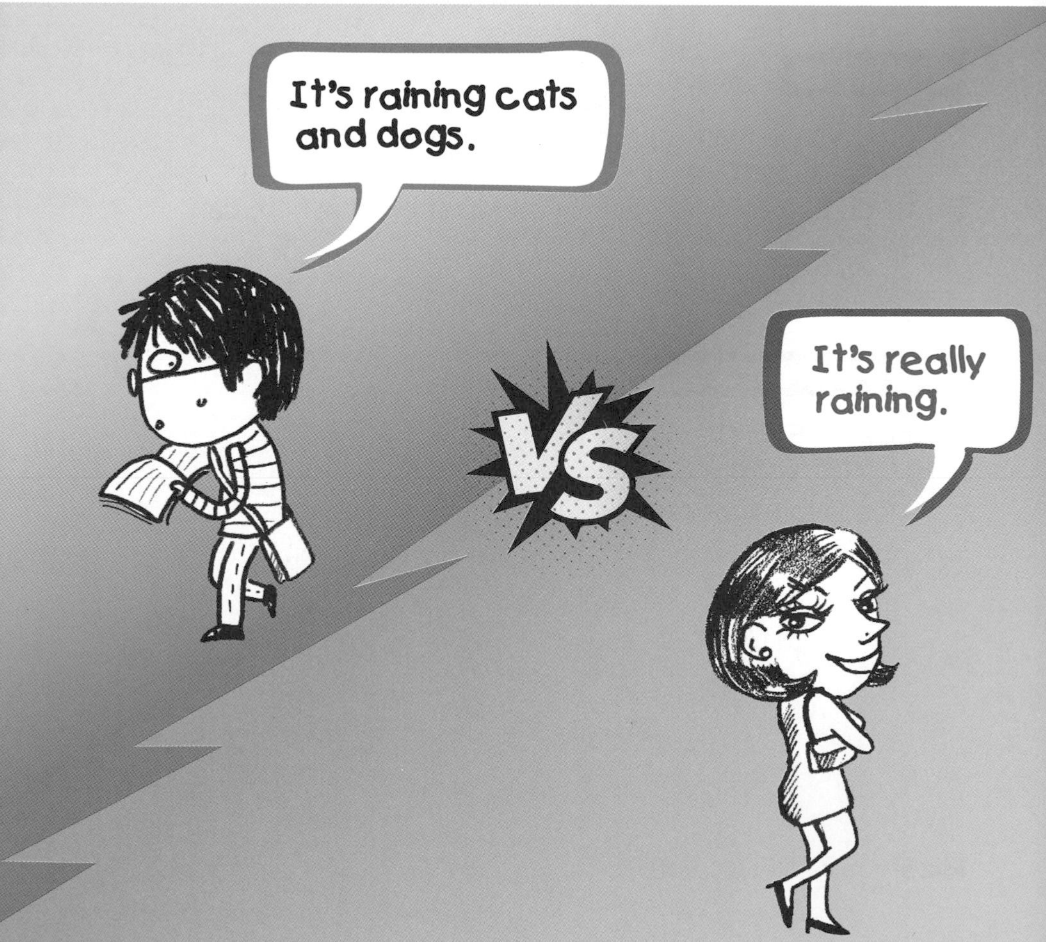

1 談論熱天

 ◀◀◀ 說法比一比 ▶▶▶

學校 **It's too hot.**
天氣太熱了。

老外 **I'm not used to this heat.**
我不習慣天氣這麼熱。

實境對話　MP3 071

Ⓐ I'm not used to this heat.
我不習慣天氣這麼熱。
Ⓑ Neither am I.
我也是。

舉一反三學起來！

- I can't believe how hot it is.
  我不敢相信會這麼熱。
- The humidity is killing me.
  濕氣真讓我受不了。
- Hot enough for you?
  夠熱了吧？

關鍵字 ▶ heat 炎熱；高溫、humidity 潮濕

2 談論冷天

學校 **I'm afraid of the cold.**
我怕冷。

老外 **I can't stand the cold.**
我受不了冷天。

實境對話 MP3 072

Ⓐ I can't stand the cold.
我受不了冷天。

Ⓑ Yeah, I have a hard time with it too.
嗯啊，我也覺得很難受。

舉一反三學起來！

● I hate cold weather.
我討厭冷天。

● I'm not used to cold weather.
我不習慣冷天。

關鍵字 ▶ can't stand 受不了、cold 冷；低溫、cold weather 冷天

3 談論雨天

 ◄◄◄ **說法比一比** ►►►

學校 **It's raining cats and dogs.**
現在下著傾盆大雨。

老外 **It's really raining.**
雨下得真大。

💬 實境對話　MP3 073

Ⓐ It's really raining.
雨下得真大。

Ⓑ Yeah, it's going to be like this all week.
是啊，整個星期都會像這個樣子。

🔑 舉一反三學起來！

● It's really coming down.
雨下得真猛。

● It's raining pretty hard.
雨下得很兇。

關鍵字 ► come down（雨）落下、hard（雨下得）猛烈地

Part 5

興趣

1 詢問對方的興趣

 ◀◀◀ 說法比一比 ▶▶▶

學校 **What is your hobby?**
你的嗜好是什麼？

老外 **What do you do for fun?**
你都做什麼娛樂？

💬 實境對話 MP3 074

A What do you do for fun?
你都做什麼娛樂？
B I like to spend time outside. Hiking, biking, that kind of stuff.
我喜歡待在戶外。健行、騎腳踏車之類的事。

舉一反三學起來！

● What do you usually do on the weekends?
週末你通常在做什麼？
● What do you like to do in your free time?
你有空時都喜歡做什麼？
● What do you do when you're not working?
你沒上班時都在做什麼？

關鍵字 ▶ for fun 為了樂趣、free time 空閒時間

99

2 談論興趣──電腦

 ◄◄◄ **說法比一比** ►►►

學校 **I usually play the computer after dinner.**
我通常會在晚餐後打電腦。

- -

老外 **I usually mess around on the computer after dinner.**
我通常會在晚餐後玩電腦。

💬 實境對話　MP3 075

A What do you usually do after work?
你下班後通常會做什麼？

B I usually mess around on the computer after dinner.
我通常會在晚餐後玩電腦。

🎵 舉一反三學起來！

- I usually spend a little time online.
  我通常會花點時間上網。
- I play a few online games.
  我會玩一些線上遊戲。
- I check email and Facebook, and check the news, too.
  我會查看一下電子郵件和臉書，還有新聞。

關鍵字 ▶ mess around 閒蕩；鬼混、online game 線上遊戲

3 談論興趣──音樂

 ◀◀◀ **說法比一比** ▶▶▶

學校 **Who's your idol?**
你的偶像是誰？

老外 **Do you have a favorite band or singer?**
你有沒有最喜歡的樂團或歌手？

實境對話 　MP3 076

A I usually listen to music on my way to work.
我通常會在上班途中聽音樂。
B Oh yeah? Do you have a favorite band or singer?
是嗎？你有沒有最喜歡的樂團或歌手？

舉一反三學起來！

- What kind of music do you like?
  你喜歡哪種音樂？
- What kind of stuff do you listen to mostly?
  你多半是聽哪種音樂？
- What have you been listening to lately?
  你最近都在聽什麼？

關鍵字 ▶ favorite 喜愛的

4 談論興趣——電影

◄◄◄ 說法比一比 ►►►

學校 **Which movie did you see recently?**
你最近看了哪部電影？

老外 **Have you seen any good movies recently?**
你最近有沒有看什麼不錯的電影？

實境對話 MP3 077

Ⓐ Have you seen any good movies recently?
你最近有沒有看什麼不錯的電影？
Ⓑ Yeah, lots.
有啊，滿多的。

舉一反三學起來！

● What's showing now?
現在在上映什麼電影？
● Have you seen *Black Widow* yet?
《黑寡婦》你看了沒？

關鍵字 ► see a movie 看電影、show 上映

5 談論興趣——運動

 ◀◀◀ **說法比一比** ▶▶▶

學校 **What's your favorite sport?**
你最喜歡的運動是什麼？

老外 **Do you follow any sports?**
你有在關注什麼運動嗎？

實境對話　MP3 078

A Do you follow any sports?
你有在關注什麼運動嗎？
B No, I'm not really into sports.
沒有，我對運動不太感興趣。

舉一反三學起來！

- Are you watching the playoffs?
你有看季後賽嗎？
- Do you follow the NBA?
你看不看美國職籃？
- Are you a soccer fan?
你是足球迷嗎？

關鍵字 ▶ follow 關注；留意、playoff 季後賽、fan 粉絲
大師提點 ▶ 在尚未確定對方是否喜歡運動前，先別急著問他的 favorite 運動是哪一個。

6 談論興趣──閱讀

學校 **Do you enjoy reading?**
你喜歡看書嗎？

- -

老外 **Do you read much?**
你看書看得多嗎？

🗨 實境對話　MP3 079

Ⓐ Do you read much?
你看書看得多嗎？

Ⓑ Not as much as I'd like to.
沒我希望的那麼多。

🎵 舉一反三學起來！

- What kind of stuff do you like to read?
  你喜歡看哪類書？
- Are you a big reader?
  你是個很愛看書的人嗎？
- Do you do a lot of reading?
  你看很多書嗎？

關鍵字 ▶ read 看書、a big reader 看很多書的人

7 談論興趣——料理

◀◀◀ 說法比一比 ▶▶▶

學校 **Can you cook?**
你會做菜嗎？

老外 **Do you like to cook?**
你喜歡做菜嗎？

實境對話　MP3 080

Ⓐ Do you like to cook?
你喜歡做菜嗎？

Ⓑ Yeah, I wish I had more time to do it.
喜歡。真希望我有更多的時間可以做。

舉一反三學起來！

● Do you cook much?
你常煮東西嗎？

● What kind of stuff do you make?
你都煮些什麼？

● Have you ever made any Chinese dishes?
你做過什麼中式料理嗎？

關鍵字 ▶ cook 煮、Chinese dish 中式料理

8 談論興趣——寵物

學校 **Do you keep a dog?**
你養狗嗎？

老外 **Do you have any pets?**
你有養什麼寵物嗎？

💬 實境對話　MP3 081

A　Do you have any pets?
　　你有養什麼寵物嗎？

B　No, my apartment is too small.
　　沒有，我的公寓太小了。

🎸 舉一反三學起來！

- Have you ever had a dog?
　你有沒有養過狗？
- Are you a cat person?
　你是貓奴嗎？

關鍵字 ► have 有（寵物）、a cat person 愛貓的人

Part 6
家庭

1 詢問對方的家中人數

◄◄◄ 說法比一比 ►►►

學校 **How many members are there in your family?**
你家有幾個成員？

老外 **How many people are there in your family?**
你家有多少人？

💬 實境對話 　MP3 082

Ⓐ How many people are there in your family?
你家有多少人？

Ⓑ Including my parents there are eight of us.
連我爸媽共八個人。

舉一反三學起來！

● Do you have a big family?
你家人很多嗎？

● Do you come from a big family?
你是來自大家庭嗎？

關鍵字 ▶ how many 多少、a big family 大家庭

2 詢問對方的兄弟姊妹

 ◀◀◀ **說法比一比** ▶▶▶

學校 **Do you have any siblings?**
你有任何兄弟姊妹嗎？

- -

老外 **Do you have any brothers or sisters?**
你有任何兄弟或姊妹嗎？

🗨 實境對話　MP3 083

Ⓐ　Do you have any brothers or sisters?
　　你有任何兄弟或姊妹嗎？
Ⓑ　No, I'm an only child.
　　沒有，我是獨生女。

🦴 舉一反三學起來！

- Is your sister older or younger?
  你的是姊姊還是妹妹？
- What does your brother do?
  令兄在哪高就？

關鍵字 ▶ only child 獨生子女

大師提點 🗣 Sibling 是比較正式的用字，通常用在寫作、而非口語。

3 詢問對方的子女

 ◄◄◄ 說法比一比 ►►►

學校 **Do you have a child?**
你有孩子嗎？

老外 **Do you have kids?**
你有小孩嗎？

實境對話 MP3 084

Ⓐ Do you have kids?
你有小孩嗎？

Ⓑ Yes. A boy, 6, and a girl, 4.
有，兒子六歲，女兒四歲。

舉一反三學起來！

● How many kids do you have?
你有幾個小孩？

● Are they in school?
他們上學了嗎？

關鍵字 ▶ kid 小孩

4 談論自己的家庭

  ◂◂◂ 說法比一比 ▸▸▸

學校 **There are five people in my family.**
我家有五個人。

老外 **Well, including my parents there are five of us.**
嗯,連我爸媽共五個人。

💬 實境對話 `MP3 085`

Ⓐ Do you have a big family?
你家人很多嗎?

Ⓑ Well, including my parents there are five of us.
嗯,連我爸媽共五個人。

🔖 舉一反三學起來!

- I've got an older sister and a younger brother.
  我有一個姊姊和一個弟弟。
- My son is 2, and we've got a little girl on the way.
  我兒子兩歲,而且我們就快有個小女兒了。

關鍵字 ▸ including 包括、older sister 姊姊、younger brother 弟弟、on the way 在途中;即將到來

5 談論自己的生活狀況

 ◀◀◀ 說法比一比 ▶▶▶

學校 **I live outside.**
我住外面。

老外 **I have my own place.**
我有自己的住處。

🗨 實境對話　MP3 086

Ⓐ Do you live at home?
你住家裡嗎？

Ⓑ No, I have my own place.
不是，我有自己的住處。

🎵 舉一反三學起來！

● I don't live with my parents.
我不跟爸媽住。

● I'm sharing a place with some friends.
我跟一些朋友一起住。

● I have a studio near my office.
我在辦公室附近有個套房。

關鍵字 ▶ share 共用、studio 套房

112

Part 7

旅遊

Have you ever been overseas?
VS
Have you ever been to another country?

1 詢問旅遊經驗

 ◀◀◀ 說法比一比 ▶▶▶

學校 **Have you ever been overseas?**
你出過國嗎？

老外 **Have you ever been to another country?**
你去過別的國家嗎？

💬 實境對話　MP3 087

A Have you ever been to another country?
你去過別的國家嗎？
B No, it's going to be my first time.
沒有，這將是我的第一次。

📎 舉一反三學起來！

● Have you ever been out of the country?
你出過國嗎？
● Have you ever traveled abroad?
你出國旅遊過嗎？

關鍵字 ▶ out of the country 出國、travel abroad 出國旅遊

2 討論行程

 ◄◄◄ **說法比一比** ►►►

學校 **I went to Japan for travel in May.**
我五月去了日本旅遊。

老外 **I went to Japan in May.**
我五月去了日本。

💬 實境對話　 MP3 088

Ⓐ What's new?
有什麼新鮮事？
Ⓑ Well, I went to Japan in May.
噢，我五月去了日本。

🎷 舉一反三學起來！

- I took a trip to Japan in May.
  我五月去了一趟日本。
- I went to Japan for a short vacation in May.
  我五月時去日本短暫渡了個假。
- My company sent me to Japan in May.
  我們公司五月時派我去了日本。

關鍵字 ▶ take a trip to 去……旅行、for a vacation 渡假

大師提點 🎷 在 went to Japan 後面加上 for travel 是多此一舉，前面的句意已經很完整。

3 描述地方

學校 **The public security is not good.**
公共治安不好。

老外 **It's not the safest place to visit.**
那不是個最安全的去處。

實境對話 MP3 089

Ⓐ What's it like there?
那裡是什麼樣子？

Ⓑ Well, it's not the safest place to visit.
嗯，那不是個最安全的去處。

舉一反三學起來！

● It's not very safe there.
那裡不太安全。

● You have to be careful there.
你在那裡得小心才行。

關鍵字 ▶ safe 安全的、careful 小心的

116

4 詢問旅遊計畫

 ◄◄◄ **說法比一比** ►►►

學校 **What country do you want to go to?**
你想去哪個國家？

- -

老外 **Where are you thinking about going on your next vacation?**
你下次渡假想去哪裡？

實境對話 **MP3 090**

Ⓐ Where are you thinking about going on your next vacation?
你下次渡假想去哪裡？

Ⓑ Well, I've always wanted to go to Portugal.
嗯，我一直想去葡萄牙。

舉一反三學起來！

- Any plans for your next vacation?
下次渡假有什麼計畫嗎？
- Is there any place that you really want to visit?
有什麼地方是你很想去的嗎？

關鍵字 ► go on a vacation 渡假、for your next vacation 為了下個假期

117

Part 8
學校／教育

1 談論自己的教育背景 **1**

 ◄◄◄ **說法比一比** ►►►

學校 **I was educated in Taiwan.**
我是在台灣受教育。

老外 **I went to school in Taiwan.**
我是在台灣上的學。

實境對話 MP3 **091**

A You're pretty good at differential equations.
你的微分方程式很強。
B Of course, I went to school in Taiwan.
當然，我是在台灣上的學。

舉一反三學起來！

- I went to university in Taiwan.
  我是在台灣讀大學。
- I got my master's degree in Taiwan.
  我是在台灣拿到碩士學位。

關鍵字 ► go to university 上大學、master's degree 碩士學位

2 談論自己的教育背景 2

 ◀◀◀ 說法比一比 ▶▶▶

學校 **I learned that when I was a junior high school student.**
我讀國中的時候學的。

老外 **I learned that in junior high.**
我是在國中學的。

實境對話 MP3 092

Ⓐ You're pretty good at chemistry.
你的化學很強。

Ⓑ Not really. I learned that in junior high.
沒有啦。我是在國中學的。

舉一反三學起來！

- We studied geometry in elementary school.
  我們在小學就讀幾何了。
- They made us take chemistry in high school.
  我們在中學時都要讀化學。
- I didn't start studying German until I was in college.
  我到了大學才開始讀德文。

關鍵字 ▶ chemistry 化學、geometry 幾何學

3 談論科系 1

 ◄◄◄ **說法比一比** ►►►

學校 **What do you major in?**
你主修什麼？

老外 **What's your major?**
你主修什麼？

💬 **實境對話** MP3 093

Ⓐ What's your major?
你主修什麼？
Ⓑ Business. I hate it.
商學。我很討厭。

✂ **舉一反三學起來！**

- What are you studying?
你是唸什麼的？
- Do you have a minor?
你有輔修嗎？

關鍵字 ► major 主修、minor 輔修

4 談論科系 2

 ◄◄◄ 說法比一比 ►►►

學校 **I graduated from Taiwan University accounting department.**
我畢業於台大會計系。

老外 **I have a degree in accounting from Taiwan University.**
我有台大的會計學位。

實境對話 MP3 094

A Were you a math major?
你主修數學嗎?

B No, I have a degree in accounting from Taiwan University.
不是,我有台大的會計學位。

舉一反三學起來!

- I studied physics in school.
  我唸書時讀的是物理。
- I majored in electrical engineering.
  我主修電機工程。
- I have a master's degree in art history.
  我有藝術史的碩士學位。

關鍵字 ▸ degree 學位、physics 物理、electrical engineering 電機工程

5 談論所學的荒廢

 ◄◄◄ 說法比一比 ►►►

學校 **I gave what I've learned back to the teacher.**
我把所學的一切都還給老師了。

老外 **I don't remember anything from my classes.**
我完全記不得上課的內容了。

實境對話 [MP3] 095

Ⓐ What year was the Yuan Dynasty founded?
元朝是哪一年創立的？

Ⓑ Are you kidding? I don't remember anything from my history classes.
你在開玩笑吧？我完全記不得歷史課的內容了。

舉一反三學起來！

● I forgot all that stuff as soon as the test was over.
考試一考完，我就什麼都忘了。

● I wish I had paid more attention in class.
要是我上課能更專心就好了。

關鍵字 ► from class 課堂上的

Part 9
工作

1 介紹自己的工作

 ◄◄◄ **說法比一比** ►►►

學校 **I'm a salesperson.**
我是個業務員。

老外 **I'm in sales.**
我是做業務的。

Ch 2

Part 9

工作

💬 實境對話　MP3 096

A What do you do?
你做哪一行？
B I'm in sales.
我是做業務的。

✍ 舉一反三學起來！

- I do sales.
我做的是業務。
- I work for an electronics manufacturer.
我在電子製造廠上班。

大師提點 💬 "I'm a/an + 職稱" 是介紹工作的標準說法，多學一些不同的說法可使口語表達更有變化。

◀◀ **說法比一比** ▶▶

學校 **I've worked for about three years in the society.**
我出社會工作了三年左右。

老外 **I've been out of school and working for about three years now.**
我離開學校到現在工作了三年左右。

💬 實境對話 MP3 097

Ⓐ Did you just graduate?
你剛畢業嗎？

Ⓑ No, I've been out of school and working for about three years now.
不是，我離開學校到現在工作了三年左右。

✂ 舉一反三學起來！

● I've been working since I graduated three years ago.
我三年前畢業後就一直在工作了。
● I was with my previous company for a year.
我在前一家公司待了一年。
● I've been with my current company for about two years now.
我待在目前這家公司至今兩年左右。

3 談論自己的工作 2

 ◄◄◄ 說法比一比 ►►►

學校 **You must have a lot of stress at work.**
你上班時一定壓力很大。

老外 **You must be under a lot of pressure at work.**
你上班時一定壓力很大。

實境對話　MP3 098

Ⓐ I'm a bonds trader.
我是個債券交易員。

Ⓑ You must be under a lot of pressure at work.
你上班時一定壓力很大。

舉一反三學起來！

- That sounds like a fairly stressful job.
  那聽起來像是個壓力很大的工作。
- That must be a pretty high-pressure job.
  那一定是壓力滿大的工作。

關鍵字 ▶ under pressure 處於壓力之下、stressful 壓力大的、high-pressure 高壓的

4 談論金錢

 ◀◀◀ **說法比一比** ▶▶▶

學校 **He's a rich man.**
他是個有錢人。

老外 **He's rich.**
他很有錢。

實境對話 MP3 099

Ⓐ Why is everyone so nice to him?
大家為什麼都對他那麼好？

Ⓑ He's rich.
他很有錢。

舉一反三學起來！

● He's got a lot of money.
他家財萬貫。

● He's doing OK for himself.
他過得不錯。

關鍵字 ▶ doing OK 過得不錯

Part 10

交通

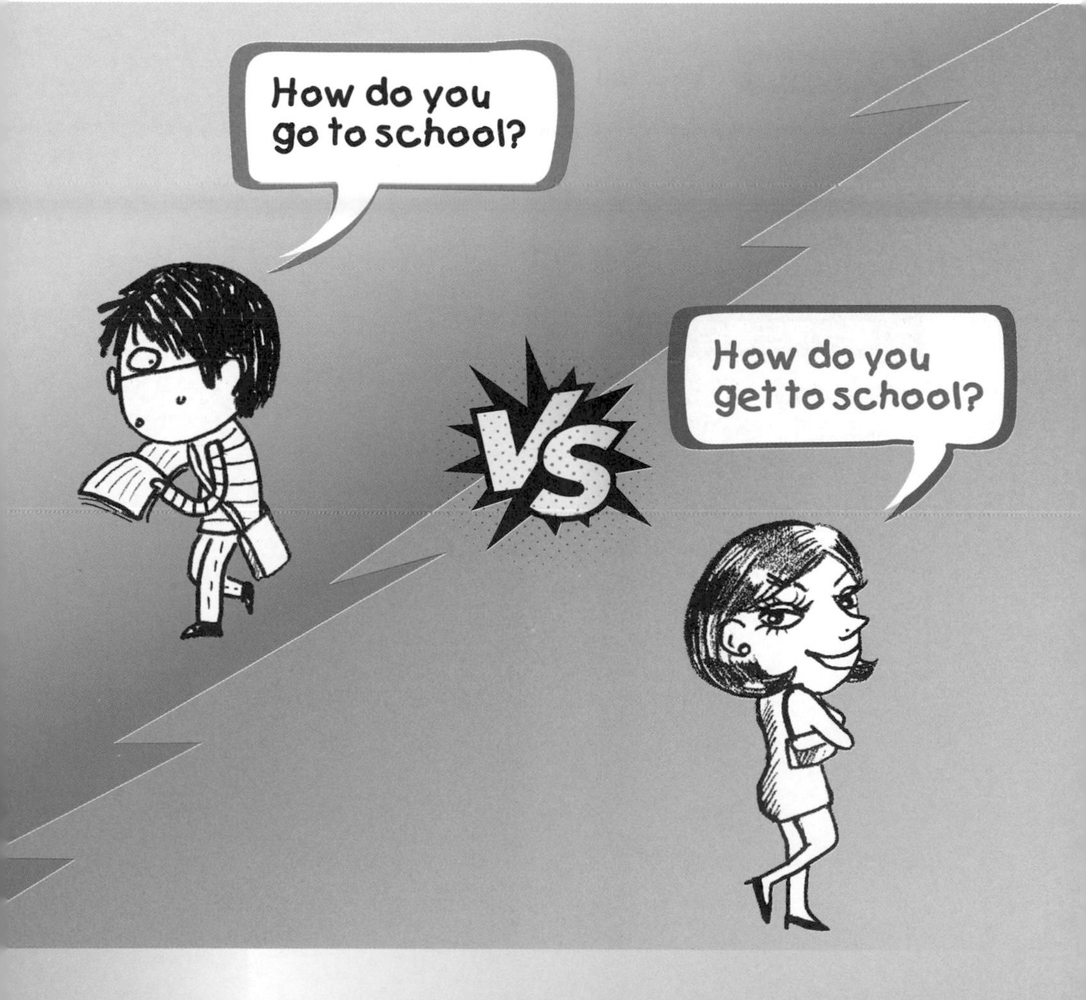

1 詢問對方的通勤方式

 ◄◄◄ 說法比一比 ▶▶▶

學校 **How do you go to school?**
你怎麼去上學？

老外 **How do you get to school?**
你怎麼去上學？

實境對話 MP3 100

Ⓐ How do you get to school?
你怎麼去上學？
Ⓑ I have a scooter.
騎機車。

舉一反三學起來！

- How do you usually get here?
  你通常是怎麼來這裡？
- Do you drive to school?
  你開車上學嗎？
- Can you bike to school from where you live?
  你可以從你住的地方騎腳踏車上學嗎？

關鍵字 ▶ scooter 輕型摩托車、drive 開車、bike 騎腳踏車

2 談論自己的通勤方式

 ◄◄◄ 說法比一比 ►►►

學校 **I go to work by bus.**
我是搭公車上班。

老外 **I take the bus to work.**
我搭公車上班。

💬 實境對話　MP3 101

Ⓐ How do you usually get here?
你通常是怎麼來這裡？

Ⓑ I always take the bus to work.
我一向是搭公車上班。

🎵 舉一反三學起來！

● There's a bus that goes right from my house to the office.
有一班公車就從我家開往辦公室。

● I usually take the MRT.
我通常是搭捷運。

● If it's raining, I'll take a cab.
假如下雨的話，我就會搭計程車。

關鍵字 ▶ take the bus 搭公車、take the MRT 搭捷運、take a cab 搭計程車

◄◄◄ 說法比一比 ►►►

學校 **I spend about twenty minutes going to school.**
我到學校大概要花二十分鐘。

老外 **It takes me about twenty minutes to get to school.**
我到學校大概要二十分鐘。

實境對話 MP3 102

Ⓐ What's your commute like?
你的通勤情況怎麼樣？

Ⓑ It takes me about twenty minutes to get to school.
我到學校大概要二十分鐘。

舉一反三學起來！

● I can get here in about twenty minutes.
我大概二十分鐘就能到這裡。

● To get to my 9 o'clock class on time, I have to leave by 8:30.
為了準時趕上九點的課，我必須在八點半以前出門。

關鍵字 ▶ commute 通勤

大師提點 發現了嗎？在這幾個談論「通勤方式」、「通勤時間」的單元，老外常用 get 而不是 go 來表達前往某個地點。

Part 11
健康和運動

1 營養

 Milk is good for our health.
牛奶對我們的健康有益。

 Milk is good for you.
牛奶對我們有益。

💬 實境對話　MP3 103

Ⓐ Why do you drink so many lattes?
你為什麼喝這麼多拿鐵？

Ⓑ Milk is good for you.
牛奶對我們有益啊。

舉一反三學起來！

- Milk is supposed to be good for your teeth.
一般認為牛奶對牙齒有益。

- Milk has lots of vitamins and minerals.
牛奶有很多維生素和礦物質。

關鍵字 ➤ good for you 對你有好處

大師提點 「對健康有益」常被逐字翻成 good for health，但其實 good for you 才是比較道地的說法。

134

2 運動時間

 ◄◄◄ 說法比一比 ►►►

學校 **I always do some exercise before breakfast.**
我一向是在早餐前做些運動。

老外 **I always exercise before breakfast.**
我一向是在早餐前運動。

實境對話 MP3 104

A Do you want to play basketball with us tonight?
你今天晚上要跟我們打籃球嗎？

B No, thanks. I always exercise before breakfast.
不了，謝謝。我一向是在早餐前運動。

舉一反三學起來！

- I only do yoga during my lunch hour.
  我只在午餐時間做瑜珈。
- I take a long walk every night after dinner.
  我每天晚餐後都會走很遠的路。

關鍵字 ▶ exercise 運動、do yoga 做瑜珈、take a long walk 走很遠的路

3 流汗

學校 **I sweat easily.**
我很容易流汗。

- -

老外 **I sweat a lot.**
我很會流汗。

🗨 實境對話 MP3 105

Ⓐ Isn't it hard to play with that towel around your neck?
脖子上掛著那條毛巾不是很難做運動嗎?

Ⓑ Yeah, but what can I do? I sweat a lot.
是啊,可是我能怎麼辦?我很會流汗。

舉一反三學起來!

- I tend to get pretty sweaty.
  我常常汗流浹背。
- I sweat like a pig.
  我流汗跟下雨一樣。

關鍵字 ▶ sweat 流汗、sweaty 汗流浹背的、sweat like a pig 汗如雨下

4 談論新冠肺炎 1

 ◀◀◀ 說法比一比 ▶▶▶

學校 **Have you downloaded that new social distancing A-P-P?**
你有下載那個新的社交距離 A-P-P 嗎？

- -

老外 **Have you downloaded that new social distancing app?**
你有下載那個新的社交距離 app 嗎？

🗨 實境對話　MP3 106

🅐 Have you downloaded that new social distancing app?
你有下載那個新的社交距離 app 嗎？

🅑 Yeah, but since I never go out, I don't know if it's working.
有啊，不過因為我都足不出戶，也不知道它有沒有用。

👆 舉一反三學起來！

- Did you ever check out that COVID-19 symptoms app?
  你有沒有試過那個新冠肺炎症狀 app？
- Have you tried that QR code messaging service?
  你試過那個掃 QR code 的簡訊實聯制服務了嗎？

關鍵字 ▶ download 下載、social distancing 保持社交距離、symptom 症狀

大師提點 🗣 說到「應用程式」，相當多台灣人會按照字母一字一字地唸出 A-P-P，不過事實上這樣的說法對只會說英語的老外而言可能會引起混淆，正確讀法為 [æp]。

5 談論新冠肺炎 2

◀◀◀ 說法比一比 ▶▶▶

學校 **I think that the staffs at the testing sites are being underpaid.**
我認為篩檢站的工作人員薪資過低。

老外 **I think that the staff at the testing sites are being underpaid.**
我認為篩檢站的工作人員薪資過低。

實境對話 MP3 107

Ⓐ I think that the staff at the testing sites are being underpaid.
我認為篩檢站的工作人員薪資過低。

Ⓑ The doctors and nurses should be paid more too.
醫護人員也應該要加薪。

舉一反三學起來！

● The frontline medical workers should all receive hazard pay.
第一線醫護人員都應該領取危險津貼。

● I really think that the nurses should be paid more.
我真的認為護理師應該得到更多的報酬。

關鍵字 ▶ testing site 篩檢站、underpaid 報酬過低的、frontline medical worker 前線醫療工作者、hazard pay 危險津貼

大師提點 "Staff" 是一個集合名詞，指的是整體，若要表達單一員工，則須使用 "worker(s)"「工作者」、"employee(s)"「僱員」、"staffer(s)" 或 "staff members"「職員」。若要說 "Staffs" 也 OK，但前提是指兩個以上不同的工作人員全體。

Part 12
感情

How long have you and your boyfriend been together?

How long have you been going out with your boyfriend?

1 討論約會對象 1

◄◄◄ 說法比一比 ►►►

學校 **Do you mind if your boyfriend is a short man?**
你介不介意你的男朋友是個矮子？

老外 **Would you ever date a short guy?**
你會跟矮子約會嗎？

實境對話　MP3 108

A Would you ever date a short guy?
你會跟矮子約會嗎？

B Sure, why not?
會啊，為什麼不？

舉一反三學起來！

● Would you go out with somebody shorter than you?
你會跟比你矮的人出去嗎？

● Would you date a woman who was older than you?
你會跟比你老的女人約會嗎？

關鍵字 ▶ date 約會、go out with 和⋯⋯約會

2 討論約會對象 2

 ◄◄◄ **說法比一比** ►►►

學校 **Do you want to make a girlfriend abroad?**
你想在國外交女朋友嗎？

老外 **Do you want to have a girlfriend while you're abroad?**
你在國外的時候，你會想交女朋友嗎？

實境對話　MP3 109

Ⓐ Do you want to have a girlfriend while you're abroad?
你在國外的時候，你會想交女朋友嗎？

Ⓑ Well, if it happens, it happens.
呣，順其自然吧。

舉一反三學起來！

- Are you hoping to meet someone while you're there?
  等你到了那裡，你會希望找個對象嗎？
- Are you going to have time to go out and maybe meet someone while you're there?
  等你到了那裡，你會有時間談戀愛，或許還能找個對象嗎？

關鍵字 ▶ abroad 在國外、meet someone 找到對象

3 討論約會對象 3

學校 **Can you accept having a foreign girlfriend?**
你能接受外國女友嗎？

老外 **Would you ever go out with someone who wasn't from Taiwan?**
你會跟外國人交往嗎？

實境對話 MP3 110

Ⓐ Would you ever go out with someone who wasn't from Taiwan?
你會跟外國人交往嗎？

Ⓑ Are you asking me to be your boyfriend?
你是要我當你男朋友嗎？

舉一反三學起來！

- Would you care if your girlfriend couldn't speak Chinese?
  你介不介意你的女朋友不會說中文？
- Does it matter where your girlfriend is from?
  你的女朋友是哪裡人會有影響嗎？

關鍵字 ▶ care 在意、matter 有關係

4 約會頻率

 ◄◄◄ 說法比一比 ►►►

學校 **How many times a week do you date with your boyfriend?**
你一星期跟你男朋友約會幾次？

老外 **How often do you go out with your boyfriend?**
你多常跟你男朋友約會？

實境對話 MP3 111

Ⓐ How often do you go out with your boyfriend?
你多常跟你男朋友約會？

Ⓑ Just once or twice a week.
一星期就這麼一、兩次。

舉一反三學起來！

- Do you and your boyfriend go out a lot?
  你很常跟你男朋友出去嗎？
- Do you see your boyfriend every day?
  你每天都會和男朋友見面嗎？

關鍵字 ► how often 多常

5 約會地點

學校 **What place in Taipei is most suitable for dating?**
台北哪個地方最適合約會？

老外 **Where's a good place to take a date in Taipei?**
台北有什麼約會的好地方？

實境對話　MP3 112

A Where's a good place to take a date in Taipei?
台北有什麼約會的好地方？

B Depends on what she likes.
要看她喜歡什麼。

舉一反三學起來！

● Where would you take someone on a first date in Taipei?
你在台北第一次約會時，會帶對方去哪裡？

● I'm going out with someone new tonight. Any suggestions?
我今天晚上要跟新對象出去。有什麼建議嗎？

關鍵字 ► take a date 帶約會對象外出、on a first date 第一次約會時

144

6 交往時間

  ◄◄◄ 說法比一比 ►►►

學校 **How long have you and your boyfriend been together?**
你跟你男朋友在一起多久了？

老外 **How long have you been going out with your boyfriend?**
你跟你男朋友交往多久了？

🗨 實境對話 ＭＰ３ 113

Ⓐ How long have you been going out with your boyfriend?
你跟你男朋友交往多久了？

Ⓑ I guess almost three years now.
我想至今大概有三年了。

舉一反三學起來！

- Have you guys been together long?
你們在一起很久了嗎？
- How long have you guys been seeing each other?
你們交往多久了？

關鍵字 ► how long 多久、see each other 交往

7 談論結婚

 ◀◀◀ **說法比一比** ▶▶▶

 Do you want to marry me?
你想和我結婚嗎？

 Do you want to get married?
你想結婚嗎？

💬 實境對話　MP3 114

Ⓐ Do you want to get married?
你想結婚嗎？

Ⓑ Hmm. Good question.
嗯，好問題。

✎ 舉一反三學起來！

● Will you marry me?
你願意嫁給我嗎？

● Do you think you guys might get married?
你覺得你們可能會結婚嗎？

● Have you thought seriously about getting married?
你們有認真考慮過結婚的事嗎？

關鍵字 ▶ get married 結婚、marry 嫁；娶

大師提點 🗣 討論結婚這件事可用 "Do you want to get married?"；求婚則說 "Will you marry me?"，用 "Do you want to marry me?" 求婚稍嫌不夠正式，甚至有點隨便。

Chapter 3

吃喝玩樂篇

Part 1
用餐

1 詢問他人的用餐選擇

 ◄◄◄ **説法比一比** ►►►

學校 **What do you want to eat?**
你想吃什麼呢？

老外 **What do you feel like?**
你想吃什麼呢？

💬 實境對話　　MP3 115

A It's almost time for lunch. What do you feel like?
午餐時間快到了，你想吃什麼呢？
B I feel like something light.
我想吃清淡的東西。

舉一反三學起來！

● What are you in the mood for?
你想吃什麼呢？

提出具體建議

● Do you feel like getting some pasta?
你想吃義大利麵嗎？
● Are you in the mood for a pizza?
你想吃披薩嗎？

關鍵字 ▶ feel like 想要、in the mood for ＋ 食物（想吃……）

2 推薦食物

 ◀◀◀ 說法比一比 ▶▶▶

學校 **Can you eat sashimi?**
你可以吃生魚片嗎？

老外 **Do you eat sashimi?**
你吃不吃生魚片？

💬 實境對話　MP3 116

Ⓐ I kind of feel like Japanese. Do you eat sashimi?
我有點想吃日本料理。你吃不吃生魚片？

Ⓑ Yeah, I love sashimi.
吃啊，我愛吃生魚片。

🎸 舉一反三學起來！

● Do you like sashimi?
你喜歡生魚片嗎？

● Is sashimi OK with you?
你可以吃生魚片嗎？

提出具體建議

● How about that new Japanese place?
那家新的日本料理店怎麼樣？

● Let's try that sushi bar near the MRT station.
我們去試試捷運站附近那家壽司吧。

關鍵字 ▶ how about＋餐廳／食物（……如何）、let's try＋餐廳／食物（讓我們試試……）

3 請人推薦餐廳

◄◄◄ **說法比一比** ►►►

學校 **Do you know any good place for steak?**
你知不知道有什麼吃牛排的好地方？

老外 **Do you know where I could get a good steak around here?**
你知不知道這附近有哪裡可以吃到不錯的牛排？

💬 **實境對話** MP3 117

Ⓐ Excuse me, do you know where I could get a good steak around here?
請問一下，你知不知道這附近有哪裡可以吃到不錯的牛排？

Ⓑ You could try BJ's. It's just down the street.
你可以去試試 BJ's。它就在這條街的街尾。

✍ **舉一反三學起來！**

● Are there any good seafood places around here?
這附近有什麼吃海鮮的好地方？

● Could you recommend a good, cheap place for lunch?
你能不能推薦一家又好又便宜的午餐店？

關鍵字 ▶ good seafood place 吃海鮮的好地方、recommend 推薦

4 表明不愛某種食物

 ◀◀◀ **說法比一比** ▶▶▶

學校 **I don't like beef.**
我不喜歡牛肉。

老外 **I don't care for beef.**
我不愛吃牛肉。

實境對話 | MP3 118

A Feel like a steak?
想吃牛排嗎？

B No, thanks. I don't care for beef.
不了，謝謝。我不愛吃牛肉。

舉一反三學起來！

- I don't eat red meat.
  我不吃紅肉。
- Anything but steak!
  除了牛排，其他都行！

關鍵字 ▶ care for 喜歡、anything but ... 除了……都可以

5 談論餐廳

  ◄◄◄ **說法比一比** ►►►

學校 **This restaurant is very famous in Taiwan.**
這家餐廳在台灣非常有名。

老外 **This place is famous for its seafood.**
這家店的海鮮很有名。

💬 實境對話　MP3 119

A It's really busy here.
生意真好。

B Yeah, this place is famous for its seafood.
是啊，這家店的海鮮很有名。

🎵 舉一反三學起來！

- This place is known for its seafood.
  這個地方是以海鮮聞名。
- This is one of the best seafood restaurants in Taiwan.
  這家店是台灣最好的海鮮餐廳之一。

關鍵字 ► famous for 以……有名、known for 以……有名

大師提點 🗣 老外鮮少只說某餐廳有名，通常會補充以何出名。

153

6 請服務生推薦菜色

 ◀◀◀ **說法比一比** ▶▶▶

〔詢問服務生〕

 What's your popular dish?
你們受歡迎的菜是什麼？

- -

 What do you recommend?
你推薦什麼？

實境對話 MP3 120

Ⓐ Are you ready to order, sir?
您準備要點餐了嗎，先生？

Ⓑ What do you recommend?
你推薦什麼？

舉一反三學起來！

- What's good here?
這裡有什麼好吃的？

請求更明確的推薦

- Do you have something that's not too oily?
你們有沒有什麼不會太油的東西？

- What do you have that's kind of light?
你們有什麼清淡一點的東西？

關鍵字 ▶ order 點餐

7 點餐

 ◀◀◀ 說法比一比 ▶▶▶

學校 **I want the spaghetti with cream sauce.**
我要奶油醬義大利麵。

老外 **I'll try the spaghetti with cream sauce.**
我要吃奶油醬義大利麵。

實境對話 MP3 121

Ⓐ What would you like?
您要吃什麼？

Ⓑ I'll try the spaghetti with cream sauce.
我要吃奶油醬義大利麵。

舉一反三學起來！

● I'd like the spaghetti with tomato sauce.
我要點蕃茄醬義大利麵。

● Could I get the spaghetti with pesto?
我可以來份青醬義大利麵嗎？

關鍵字 ▶ try 試、would like 想要、get 來份（食物）

8 點飲料

 ◀◀◀ 說法比一比 ▶▶▶

學校 **One glass of red wine, please.**
一杯紅酒，麻煩你。

老外 **A glass of red wine, please.**
一杯紅酒，麻煩你。

💬 實境對話　MP3 122

A And to drink?
飲料呢？

B A glass of red wine, please.
一杯紅酒，麻煩你。

🎙 舉一反三學起來！

● Just water, please.
開水就好，麻煩你。

● What kind of juice do you have?
你們有哪種果汁？

● I'll have a lemonade with no ice, please.
我要檸檬水去冰，麻煩你。

關鍵字 ▶ with no ice 不加冰

大師提點🗣：非母語人士會用 one 來表示「數量」，其實老外通常用 a。只有在特別強調「只要一個」而非二個、三個……時，才會用 one。

9 形容餐點──用餐前

學校 **That smells good.**
那聞起來不錯。

老外 **That looks good.**
那看起來不錯。

💬 **實境對話** `MP3` 123

A Here's your steak.
您的牛排來了。

B That looks good.
那看起來不錯。

🔖 **舉一反三學起來！**

● That smells wonderful.
那聞起來很棒。

● I'm going to need help finishing this.
我得找人幫忙才吃得完這道。

大師提點 📣 "That smells good." 是正確的英文慣用語。當食物特別香的時候，儘管這麼用無妨。但在食物端上桌脫口而出時，老外更常說的是 "That looks good."。

157

10 開始用餐

學校 **Please eat first.**
請先用。

- -

老外 **Please, go ahead. Don't wait for me.**
請先用。別等我了。

💬 實境對話　MP3 124

Ⓐ Please, go ahead. Don't wait for me.
請先用。別等我了。

Ⓑ Oh, OK. I guess I'd better start while it's still hot.
噢，好。我想我最好趁熱開動。

舉一反三學起來！

- You'd better start before it gets cold.
  你最好在它變涼以前開動。
- Dig in.
  吃吧。

先開動

- I'm sorry. I'm starving. I'm going to start first.
  抱歉，我餓了，我要先開動了。

關鍵字 ▶ go ahead 先用、start 開動

11 形容餐點──用餐後

 ◄◄◄ 說法比一比 ►►►

學校 **The dishes are delicious.**
菜很好吃。

老外 **Everything is really great.**
每道都棒極了。

🗨 **實境對話** MP3 125

A How are you enjoying your dinner?
你的晚餐吃得怎麼樣？
B Everything is really great.
每道都棒極了。

✎ **舉一反三學起來！**

- I love the chicken.
  我愛雞肉。
- The fish is fantastic.
  魚肉真棒。

關鍵字 ▶ great 很棒、love 愛、fantastic 棒極了

大師提點 🗨 形容食物美味時，非母語人士直覺會用 delicious 這個字，不過老外反而不常用。

12 處理用餐問題

◄◄◄ **說法比一比** ►►►

學校 **Can I get a new one?**
我能換個新的嗎？

老外 **Can I get another one?**
可以再給我一副嗎？

🗨 實境對話 MP3 126

Ⓐ Excuse me. I dropped my fork. Can I get another one?
不好意思，我的叉子掉了。可以再給我一支嗎？

Ⓑ Sure. I'll be right back with one.
沒問題，我馬上拿一支來。

✍ 舉一反三學起來！

● Could you give me another fork?
你能再給我一支叉子嗎？

● Can I have another knife, please?
可以麻煩你再拿支刀子來嗎？

● I need a spoon.
我需要一根湯匙。

關鍵字 ➤ another 另一個、fork 叉子、knife 刀子、spoon 湯匙

大師提點 🗨 此處要的不是全新 (new) 的叉子，所以 another（另一支）是比較精確的說法。

13 表示吃飽了

 ◄◄ **說法比一比** ►►

學校 **I'm full.**
我吃飽了。

老外 **I'm stuffed.**
我飽了。

💬 **實境對話** MP3 127

Ⓐ Did you save any room for dessert?
你有沒有留點胃來吃甜點？

Ⓑ No, thanks. I'm stuffed.
不，謝謝。我飽了。

🎸 **舉一反三學起來！**

● I can't eat another bite.
我一口都吃不下了。

詢問他人

● Did you get enough?
你有沒有吃飽？

● Should we get something else?
我們要不要吃點別的？

關鍵字 ➤ stuffed 飽了、can't eat another bite 一口都吃不下了

14 結帳

◄◄◄ 說法比一比 ►►►

學校 **Check, please.**
麻煩結帳。

老外 **Could we have the check, please?**
可以麻煩把帳單給我們嗎？

💬 實境對話　MP3 128

A Excuse me. Could we have the check, please?
　　不好意思，可以麻煩把帳單給我們嗎？

B Sure. I'll take that for you whenever you're ready.
　　沒問題。只要您準備好，我就把它拿來。

🎵 舉一反三學起來！

- We'd like the bill, please.
  我們要買單了，麻煩你。
- We're ready to go.
  我們要走了。
- Do we pay here or at the register?
  我們要在這裡還是收銀台付帳？

關鍵字 ► check 帳單、bill 帳單、register 收銀台

15 請客

 ◀◀◀ 說法比一比 ▶▶▶

學校 **Let me pay the bill.**
我來買單。

老外 **Let me get this.**
這頓我請。

實境對話 MP3 129

Ⓐ Let me get this.
這頓我請。

Ⓑ Oh, OK. I'll get the tip.
噢，好。小費我出。

舉一反三學起來！

- This one is on me.
  這頓算我的。
- Why don't you get it next time?
  你何不下次請就好？
- Don't even think about it.
  連想都別想。

關鍵字 ▶ get this 負責這個、on me 算我的

163

16 評論價格

學校 **It was too expensive.**
太貴了。

老外 **It was overpriced.**
太貴了。

💬 實境對話 MP3 130

A That was good, wasn't it?
還不錯，對吧？

B Yeah, but I think it was overpriced.
是啊，可是我覺得貴了點。

舉一反三學起來！

● That was a rip-off.
那簡直是坑人。

當價格合理時

● That was a really good deal.
真的很划算。

● I can't believe how reasonable that was.
我不敢相信會這麼公道。

關鍵字 ▶ overpriced 太貴、rip-off 敲竹槓、a good deal 很划算、reasonable 合理的

Part 2

購物

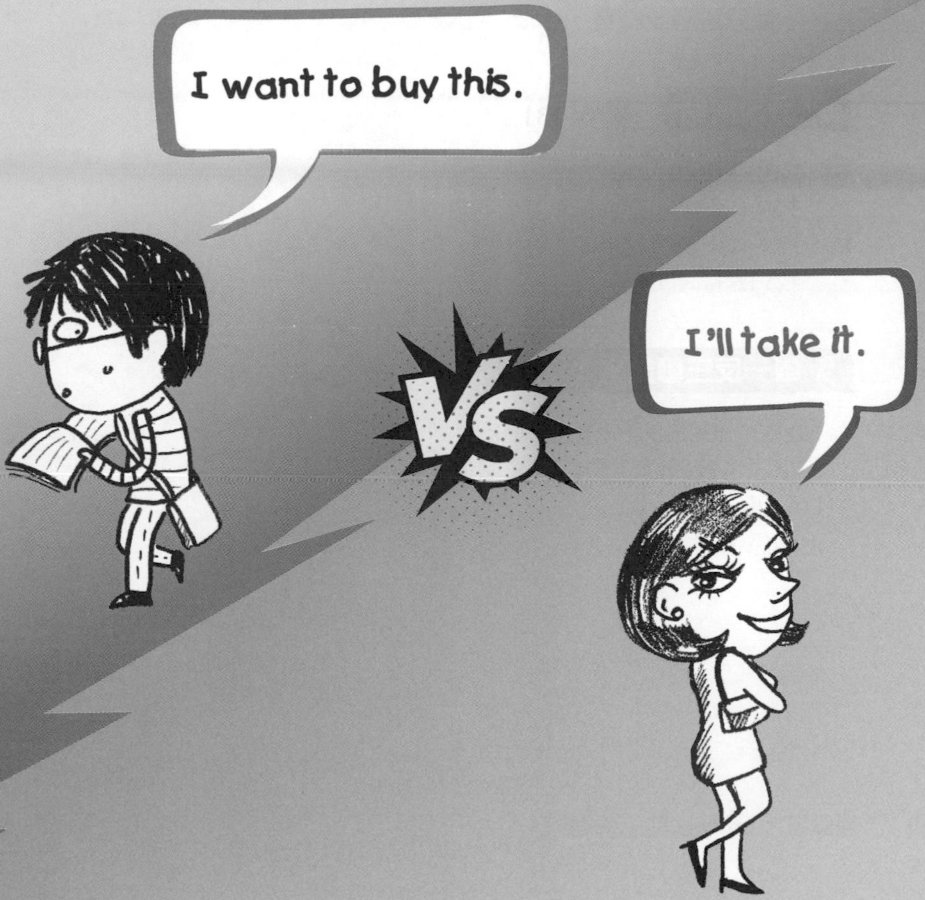

1 婉拒店員的協助

 ◄◄◄ **說法比一比** ►►►

[Can I help you?]
學校 **No, thank you.**
不用了，謝謝。

[Can I help you?]
老外 **I'm just browsing.**
我只是隨便看看。

實境對話　MP3 131

Ⓐ Can I help you?
我可以為您效勞嗎？

Ⓑ I'm just browsing.
我只是隨便看看。

舉一反三學起來！

- No, I'm just looking, thanks.
  不用了，我只是隨便看看，謝謝。
- I'm OK, thanks.
  沒關係，謝謝。

關鍵字 ► browse 隨意看看

2 表明要找什麼

 ◀◀◀ **說法比一比** ▶▶▶

學校 **I need a new pair of jeans.**
我需要一條牛仔褲。

老外 **I'm looking for some jeans.**
我在找牛仔褲。

🗨 **實境對話** MP3 132

Ch 3

Part 2

購
物

Ⓐ Is there anything I can help you with?
有沒有什麼我可以為您效勞的？

Ⓑ Yeah, I'm looking for some jeans.
有，我在找牛仔褲。

✎ **舉一反三學起來！**

● I'm looking for something fun and sexy.
我在找有趣又性感的東西。

● Do you have any business casual stuff?
你們有沒有什麼上班族的休閒款式？

關鍵字 ▶ look for 找、business casual 上班族休閒的

3 詢問是否有貨

學校 **Do you have Levi's?**
你們有沒有 Levi's？

老外 **Do you carry Levi's?**
你們有賣 Levi's 嗎？

實境對話　MP3 133

A These Prada jeans are on sale for only $189.99.
這件 Prada 牛仔褲在特價，只賣 189.99 美元。

B Do you carry Levi's?
你們有賣 Levi's 嗎？

舉一反三學起來！

● Do you sell Levi's?
你們有沒有賣 Levi's？
● What other brands do you carry?
你們有賣什麼別的牌子？

關鍵字 ➤ carry（商店）備有……出售、sell 賣

4 尺寸 1

 ◀◀◀ **說法比一比** ▶▶▶

學校 **Do you have an M size?**
你們有 M 號的嗎？

- -

老外 **Do you have this in a medium?**
你們有這件的 M 號嗎？

🗨 **實境對話** **MP3** 134

Ⓐ Do you have this in a medium?
你們有這件的 M 號嗎？
Ⓑ Let me go check in the back.
我去後面確認看看。

📞 **舉一反三學起來！**

● Do you have this in a smaller size?
你們有這件比較小號的嗎？
● Does this come in large?
這有大號的嗎？
● What sizes does this come in?
這有出什麼尺寸？

關鍵字 ▶ in a medium M 號的、come in + 尺寸／顏色（有……尺寸、顏色）

5 尺寸 2

學校 **My size is 4.**
我的尺寸是四號。

老外 **I'm a 4.**
我是四號。

實境對話　MP3 135

Ⓐ What size are you?
您是什麼尺寸？

Ⓑ I'm a 4.
我是四號。

舉一反三學起來！

- Do you have this in a 2?
  你們有這件的二號嗎？
- I'm a size 8.
  我是八號。
- Sometimes I can fit into a 6.
  有時候我會穿到六號。

關鍵字 ➤ fit into 穿上

6 顏色

學校 **Do you have a red one?**
你們有紅色的嗎？

- -

老外 **Does this come in red?**
這有紅色的嗎？

實境對話 MP3 136

A Does this come in red?
這有紅色的嗎？

B No, sorry. Just purple and pink.
沒有，抱歉。只有紫色跟粉紅色的。

舉一反三學起來！

● Is this the only color these come in?
這些只有這種顏色的嗎？

● What other colors does this come in?
這件有什麼別的顏色？

● Does this come in any other colors?
這件有沒有什麼別的顏色？

7 樣式

 ◀◀◀ **說法比一比** ▶▶▶

學校 **Do you have this with a flower design?**
你們這件有花朵圖案的嗎？

老外 **Do you have this in a floral print?**
你們這件有花朵圖案的嗎？

實境對話 MP3 137

Ⓐ Do you have this in a floral print?
你們這件有花朵圖案的嗎？

Ⓑ No, just the leopard print. Sorry.
沒有，只有豹紋圖案的。抱歉。

舉一反三學起來！

- Do you have this in plaid?
你們這件有格紋的嗎？
- Does this come in polka dots?
這件有圓點的嗎？
- Do you have any with stripes?
你們有沒有什麼條紋的？

關鍵字 ▶ floral print 花紋、leopard print 豹紋、plaid 格紋、polka dot 圓點、stripe 條紋

8 質料

 ◀◀◀ 說法比一比 ▶▶▶

學校 **Is this made of 100% cotton?**
這是純棉做的嗎？

老外 **Is this 100% cotton?**
這是純棉的嗎？

💬 **實境對話** MP3 138

A Is this 100% cotton?
這是純棉的嗎？

B It's a cotton-polyester blend.
是棉跟聚酯纖維混紡的。

✎ **舉一反三學起來！**

● What material is this?
這是什麼質料的？
● What is this made out of?
這是用什麼做的？
● Is this real leather?
這是真皮的嗎？

關鍵字 ▶ cotton 棉、material 質料、real leather 真皮

9 穿搭

 ◄◄◄ **說法比一比** ►►►

學校 **Do these pants match my shoes?**
這條褲子跟我的鞋子搭不搭？

老外 **Do these pants go with my shoes?**
這條褲子跟我的鞋子搭不搭？

實境對話 MP3 139

A Do these pants go with my shoes?
這條褲子跟我的鞋子搭不搭？

B Yeah, but they don't go with your socks.
搭，可是跟您的襪子不搭。

舉一反三學起來！

- Do these shoes and pants go together?
  這雙鞋和褲子搭不搭？
- Do these pants clash with my shoes?
  這條褲子會不會跟我的鞋子不搭？

關鍵字 ▶ go with 搭、go together 搭、clash with 和……不相配

174

10 詢問何時有貨

  ◀◀◀ 說法比一比 ▶▶▶

學校 [Sorry, we're out of stock.] **When will you have it?**
〔對不起，我們缺貨。〕你們什麼時候會有貨？

老外 [Sorry, we're out of stock.] **When will you get it in?**
〔對不起，我們缺貨。〕你們什麼時候會進貨？

🗨 實境對話　MP3 140

Ⓐ When will you get it in?
　你們什麼時候會進貨？

Ⓑ Try coming back on Wednesday.
　不妨星期三回來看看。

⑧ 舉一反三學起來！

● Will you be getting any more in?
　你們還會再進貨嗎？

● Do you have anything similar?
　你們有什麼類似的嗎？

關鍵字 ▶ get it in 進貨

175

◄◄◄ **說法比一比** ►►►

 I want to try this on.
我想要試這件。

 I'd like to try this on.
我想試穿這件。

🗨 **實境對話** MP3 141

Ⓐ I'd like to try this on.
我想試穿這件。

Ⓑ Sure, the dressing rooms are right over there.
好的,試衣間就在那邊。

✂ **舉一反三學起來!**

● Can I try this on?
我可以試穿這件嗎?

● I'd like to see how this fits.
我想看看這件合不合身。

● Where are the dressing rooms?
試衣間在哪裡?

關鍵字 ► try this on 試穿這件、dressing room 試衣間、fit 合身

176

12 不合身 1

學校 **It's too small.**
太小了。

老外 **It's tight in the shoulders.**
肩膀的地方緊緊的。

💬 實境對話　MP3 142

A Does it fit?
合身嗎？

B Well, it's tight in the shoulders.
呣，肩膀的地方緊緊的。

🔗 舉一反三學起來！

- It's a little too small in the seat.
  屁股的地方太小了一點。
- Ugh. I can't breathe in these.
  呃，我穿上這件就不能呼吸了。
- My toes are a bit squished.
  我的腳趾頭緊了點。

關鍵字 ▶ it's tight in + 部位（某部位緊緊的）、squished 被擠扁的

大師提點 🗣 光用 small 來說明合身程度太過籠統，不妨加上「部位」讓意思表達更清楚。

13 不合身 2

 ◀◀◀ 說法比一比 ▶▶▶

學校 **It's too big.**
太大了。

老外 **It's a little baggy.**
太寬鬆了點。

 實境對話 **MP3** 143

A Well, what do you think?
呣,你覺得怎麼樣?

B It's a little baggy.
太寬鬆了點。

舉一反三學起來!

● It feels a little loose.
感覺鬆了點。

● Do you do alterations?
你們有在幫人修改嗎?

● Can you take these in?
你們可以改小嗎?

關鍵字 ▶ baggy 寬鬆的、loose 鬆的、do alterations 修改、take these in 改小(腰圍、胸圍等)

14 殺價

學校 **Do you have any discount?**
有任何折扣嗎？

老外 **Do you have any specials?**
你們有什麼優惠嗎？

💬 **實境對話** 　MP3 144

Ⓐ　Do you have any specials?
　　你們有什麼優惠嗎？

Ⓑ　Everything on these two racks is 15% off today.
　　這兩個架上的東西今天一律八五折。

✂ **舉一反三學起來！**

● Are these on sale?
　這些在特價嗎？

● Is there a discount if I sign up for a credit card?
　假如我申請信用卡，有沒有打折？

● Is there any kind of discount if I buy three?
　假如我買三件，有沒有折扣？

關鍵字 ► special 優惠、on sale 特價的、discount 折扣

15 表明要買

學校 **I want to buy this.**
我要買這件。

老外 **I'll take it.**
我買了。

🗨 **實境對話** `MP3` 145

Ⓐ You look so cute in that!
你穿那件看起來真可愛！

Ⓑ Thanks! I'll take it.
謝謝！我買了。

✍ **舉一反三學起來！**

● Excuse me, we're ready to check out.
不好意思，我們準備要結帳了。

● Can you ring me up, please?
可以麻煩你幫我結帳嗎？

● Where can I pay for this?
我這件要去哪裡付帳？

關鍵字 ► take it 買這件、check out 結帳、ring me up 幫我結帳

16 表明不買

 ◄◄◄ 說法比一比 ►►►

學校 **No, I don't want it.**
不,我不想要。

老外 **Thanks, but I'm going to think about it.**
謝謝,但我要考慮一下。

💬 實境對話　[MP3] 146

Ⓐ Can I take that up to the register for you?
我可以幫您把那件拿去收銀台了嗎?

Ⓑ Thanks, but I'm going to think about it.
謝謝,但我要考慮一下。

✍ 舉一反三學起來!

● It's nice, but just a little out of my budget.
它是不錯,只不過有點超出了我的預算。

● Thanks, but I think I'll pass.
謝謝,但我想還是算了。

關鍵字 ▶ think about it 考慮一下、out of my budget 超出我的預算、pass
算了

17 結帳

學校 **Can I pay with my Visa card?**
可以刷 Visa 卡付款嗎？

老外 **Do you take Visa?**
你們收不收 Visa 卡？

實境對話　MP3 147

Ⓐ Would you like to put that on your Macy's card?
您那件要刷梅西卡嗎？

Ⓑ Do you take Visa?
你們收不收 Visa 卡？

舉一反三學起來！

- Do you take traveler's checks?
  你們收不收旅行支票？
- Do you take debit cards?
  你們收不收簽帳卡？
- I'll pay cash.
  我付現。

關鍵字 ▶ take 收（信用卡、貨幣等）、traveler's check 旅行支票、debit card 簽帳卡

18 退換貨

  ◀◀◀ 說法比一比 ▶▶▶

學校 **I want to exchange it.**
我想要換這件。

老外 **I'd like to exchange this, please.**
這件我想要換貨，麻煩你。

實境對話　MP3 148

Ⓐ I'd like to exchange this, please.
這件我想要換貨，麻煩你。

Ⓑ Sure. Do you have your receipt?
好的。您有帶收據嗎？

舉一反三學起來！

- I'd like to exchange this for a smaller size.
我想把這件換成比較小號的。
- I'd like to return this.
我想退掉這件。
- I don't want to exchange it. I'd like a refund, please.
我不想換貨。我想退款，麻煩你。

關鍵字 ▶ exchange 換、return 退、refund 退款

大師提點 當要表明就是手上拿的這件時，this 是比 it 更精確的說法。

Part 3
旅行

1 查驗護照——國籍

◀◀◀ 說法比一比 ▶▶▶

[Are you an American citizen?]

學校 **No, I am a Taiwanese.**
不是，我是個台灣人。

[Are you an American citizen?]

老外 **No, I'm from Taiwan.**
不是，我從台灣來的。

💬 實境對話　MP3 149

Ⓐ Are you an American citizen?
　你是美國公民嗎？

Ⓑ No, I'm from Taiwan.
　不是，我從台灣來的。

🎷 舉一反三學起來！

- No, I'm Taiwanese.
　不是，我是台灣人。
- I have dual citizenship—Taiwan and Canada.
　我有雙重國籍——台灣和加拿大。

關鍵字 ▶ from 從……來的、dual citizenship 雙重國籍

2 查驗護照──入境目的（出差）

 ◄◄◄ 說法比一比 ►►►

[What is the purpose of your visit?]

學校 **I come for business.**
我來出差。

[What is the purpose of your visit?]

老外 **I'm here on business.**
我來這裡出差。

實境對話 MP3 150

A What is the purpose of your visit?
你的入境目的是什麼？

B I'm here on business.
我來這裡出差。

舉一反三學起來！

● I'm attending a training seminar.
我要參加訓練研討會。

● I'm here to see some clients.
我來這裡拜訪一些客戶。

● I'm here for the consumer electronics show in Las Vegas.
我來這裡參加拉斯維加斯的消費電子用品展。

關鍵字 ► on business 出差、attend 出席；參加、see some clients 拜訪一些客戶

3 查驗護照──入境目的（玩樂）

[What is the purpose of your visit?]

學校 I want to visit my friend.
我想來拜訪朋友。

[What is the purpose of your visit?]

老外 I'm here to see friends.
我來這裡探望朋友。

💬 實境對話　MP3 151

Ⓐ What is the purpose of your visit?
你的入境目的是什麼？

Ⓑ I'm here to see friends.
我來這裡探望朋友。

🔑 舉一反三學起來！

● I'm here on vacation.
我來這裡渡假。

● We're going to do some sightseeing.
我們是來觀光的。

● We're going to go to Disneyland.
我們要去迪士尼樂園。

關鍵字 ▶ see 探望；拜訪、on vacation 渡假、sightseeing 觀光

大師提點 🗨 發現了沒，前一個單元的「拜訪客戶」和本單元的「探望朋友」都是用 see 這個動詞，而不是 visit。

4 行李遺失、損壞

◂◂◂ 說法比一比 ▸▸▸

學校 **I lost something from my suitcase.**
我的手提箱裡有東西掉了。

老外 **Something was stolen from my suitcase.**
我的手提箱裡有東西被偷了。

💬 實境對話　MP3 152

Ⓐ What seems to be the matter, sir?
怎麼回事，先生？

Ⓑ Something was stolen from my suitcase.
我的手提箱裡有東西被偷了。

舉一反三學起來！

● I was robbed.
我被搶了。
● My bags haven't arrived.
我的包包沒有到。
● My luggage is damaged.
我的行李有損壞。

關鍵字 ▸ suitcase 手提箱、luggage 行李、damaged 損壞的

5 搭計程車去飯店

學校 **We're living at the Sheraton.**
我們要住宿喜來登。

老外 **We're staying at the Sheraton.**
我們住宿在喜來登。

實境對話　MP3 153

Ⓐ Where to, ma'am?
要去哪，女士？
Ⓑ We're staying at the Sheraton.
我們住宿在喜來登。

舉一反三學起來！

● The Hilton, please.
麻煩去希爾頓。
● Do you know where the Hyatt is?
你知道君悅在哪裡嗎？

關鍵字 ▶ stay at 住宿在……

大師提點 Live 指的是「長期居住」；stay 則是「短期停留」。

6 給計程車司機小費

學校 **Here's a tip for you.**
這是給你的小費。

老外 **This is for you.**
這是給你的。

💬 實境對話　MP3 154

A That'll be $35.
一共 35 美元。

B OK, and this is for you.
好，另外這是給你的。

✂ 舉一反三學起來！

- Please keep the change.
不用找了。
- Thank you very much.
非常感謝。

關鍵字 ▶ tip 小費、change 零錢

7 入住飯店

 ◄◄◄ 說法比一比 ►►►

學校 **I'm Liu. I reserved a room.**
我姓劉。我訂了房間。

老外 **I have a reservation under Liu, L-I-U.**
我有訂房,登記姓劉,L-I-U。

💬 實境對話 **MP3 155**

Ⓐ Welcome to the Chicago Sheraton.
歡迎光臨芝加哥喜來登。

Ⓑ Thanks, I have a reservation under Liu, L-I-U.
謝謝。我有訂房,登記姓劉,L-I-U。

举一反三学起來!

● I have a reservation. My last name is Chen.
我有訂房,我姓陳。

● I don't have a reservation. Do you have any singles available?
我沒有訂房。你們有沒有任何空的單人房?

關鍵字 ► reservation 預約、single 單人房、available 空的

191

8 買火車票 1

 ◀◀◀ 說法比一比 ▶▶▶

學校 **How can I go to Hakone?**
我可以怎麼去箱根？

老外 **How do I get to Hakone from here?**
我從這裡要怎麼去箱根？

🗨 實境對話　MP3 156

Ⓐ Excuse me, how do I get to Hakone from here?
請問一下，我從這裡要怎麼去箱根？

Ⓑ There's an express train leaving in 20 minutes.
有一班直達車會在 20 分鐘後開。

🎷 舉一反三學起來！

● What's the best way to get to Hakone?
去箱根最好的方法是什麼？

● Can I get an express train to Hakone from here?
我可以從這裡搭特快車去箱根嗎？

● Do I have to transfer?
我要轉車嗎？

關鍵字 ▶ express train 特快車；直達車、transfer 轉乘

大師提點 🎷 Go 是學校教的標準用字，下次試試改用 get，可以讓你的英文聽起來更自然。

9 買火車票 2

 ◄◄◄ 說法比一比 ►►►

學校 **How to buy a ticket from the machine?**
要怎麼用售票機買票？

老外 **Can you show me how to buy a ticket from the machine?**
你能不能教我怎麼用售票機買票？

實境對話 MP3 157

Ⓐ Problem, sir?
有問題嗎，先生？

Ⓑ Yeah, can you show me how to buy a ticket from the machine?
嗯，你能不能教我怎麼用售票機買票？

舉一反三舉起來！

- Can you show me how the ticket machine works?
  你能不能教我售票機要怎麼用？
- Can you show me how to use the ticket machine?
  你能不能教我要怎麼用售票機？

關鍵字 ► show 示範、ticket machine 售票機

193

◀◀◀ **說法比一比** ▶▶▶

學校 **Where is a 7-11 in this area?**
這附近哪裡有 7-11？

老外 **Is there a 7-11 around here?**
這附近有 7-11 嗎？

🗨 **實境對話** MP3 158

Ⓐ Is there a 7-11 around here?
這附近有 7-11 嗎？

Ⓑ Yeah, there's one right around the corner.
有啊，轉角就有一間。

✂ **舉一反三學起來！**

● Where's the nearest 7-11?
最近的 7-11 在哪裡？

● Do you know if there's a 7-11 near here?
你知道這附近有沒有 7-11 嗎？

● Is there a convenience store around here?
這附近有便利商店嗎？

大師提點 🗨 非母語人士在詢問地點時，第一反應常是用 where is 來開頭，但在此情境下，老外其實更常用 is there ... 問句。

11 提議——地方

 ◄◄◄ 說法比一比 ►►►

學校 **The hot springs are good for relaxing.**
溫泉有助於放鬆。

老外 **The hot springs are very relaxing.**
溫泉讓人非常放鬆。

💬 實境對話　MP3 159

🅐 What do you want to do tomorrow?
你明天想幹嘛？

🅑 The hot springs are very relaxing.
溫泉讓人非常放鬆。

🎧 舉一反三學起來！

- The museums are all pretty boring.
  博物館都滿無聊的。
- The beach is good for people watching.
  海邊適合觀賞人群。
- The botanical garden is worth checking out.
  植物園值得一看。

關鍵字 ▶ hot spring 溫泉、relaxing 讓人放鬆的、museum 博物館、botanical garden 植物園

12 提議──天氣

學校 **If the weather isn't fine, you might have to change your plans.**
假如天候不佳,你們可能就必須更改計畫。

老外 **If the weather isn't good, you might have to change your plans.**
假如天氣不好,你們可能就必須更改計畫。

實境對話　MP3 160

Ⓐ We'll probably go to the botanical garden.
我們大概會去植物園。

Ⓑ OK, but if the weather isn't good, you might have to change your plans.
好的,但假如天氣不好,你們可能就必須更改計畫。

舉一反三學起來!

- If it rains, you could go to the art museum.
  假如下雨,你們可以去美術館。
- If it's really hot tomorrow, you might want to check out the mall.
  假如明天真的很熱的話,你們可能會想去賣場逛逛。
- It's not really that nice at the beach when it's this windy.
  風這麼大的時候,去海邊其實沒什麼好。

大師提點 教科書和字典都可看到用 fine 來形容天氣,但這是較古老的英文,現在老外已漸漸不這麼說了。

13 提議——行前準備 1

 ◀◀ 說法比一比 ▶▶

學校 **I suggest that you prepare gloves and a warm hat.**
我建議你們準備手套和保暖帽。

老外 **You should bring gloves and a warm hat.**
你們應該要帶手套和保暖帽。

實境對話 MP3 161

Ⓐ What's the weather like at the top of the mountain?
山頂的天氣是什麼樣子？

Ⓑ It can get really cold. You should bring gloves and a warm hat.
可能會相當冷。你們應該要帶手套和保暖帽。

舉一反三學起來！

- You should definitely bring some sunblock.
  你們絕對要帶一些防曬的東西。
- Take some water with you.
  身上要帶一些水。

大師提點 「準備」常被直譯為 prepare，但此處乃提醒對方要「帶」某件物品，所以用動詞 bring。Prepare 意指花時間準備某件事，如 prepare for a test「準備考試」。

14 提議──行前準備 2

學校 **It will be a pity if you don't bring your camera.**
假如你沒帶相機，會很可惜。

老外 **It would be a shame not to bring your camera.**
沒帶相機會很可惜。

實境對話 MP3 162

Ⓐ I think I'm going to leave my bag in the hotel room.
我想我會把包包留在飯店房間裡。

Ⓑ OK, but it would be a shame not to bring your camera.
好，可是沒帶相機會很可惜。

舉一反三學起來！

● If you don't bring your camera, you'll regret it.
假如你沒帶相機，你會後悔的。

● Don't forget to bring a camera.
別忘了帶相機。

關鍵字 ▶ shame 惋惜、bring 帶、camera 相機

15 觀光

 ◄◄◄ 說法比一比 ►►►

學校 **The night view is very beautiful.**
夜景很美。

老外 **The view at night is very beautiful.**
夜景很美。

🗨 實境對話　MP3 163

A Should we go up to the Sky Lounge for a drink?
我們要不要上去雲月舫喝一杯？

B Sure, the view at night is very beautiful.
好啊，夜景很美。

🎵 舉一反三學起來！

● The view at sunset is spectacular.
日落的景色很壯觀。

● It's got a great view.
它的景色很棒。

● You can see the whole city from up there.
你從上面那裡可以看到整個城市。

關鍵字 ▶ view 景色、spectacular 壯觀的

16 拍照

學校 **Could you take a picture for me?**
你能不能幫我拍張照？

老外 **Could you take our picture?**
你能不能幫我們拍張照？

💬 實境對話　MP3 164

Ⓐ Excuse me, could you take our picture?
不好意思，你能不能幫我們拍張照？

Ⓑ Sure, no problem.
好啊，沒問題。

🎤 舉一反三學起來！

● Could you take a picture of us?
你可以幫我們拍張照嗎？

● Would you mind taking our picture?
你介意幫我們拍張照嗎？

關鍵字 ▶ take our picture / take a picture of us 幫我們照相

200

17 退房──帳單問題

  ◄◄◄ 說法比一比 ►►►

學校 **Could you tell me what this $8 is about?**
你能不能告訴我這八美元是關於什麼？

老外 **Could you tell me what this $8 is for?**
你能不能告訴我這八美元是什麼的費用？

實境對話 MP3 165

Ⓐ Excuse me, could you tell me what this $8 is for?
不好意思，你能不能告訴我這八美元是什麼的費用？

Ⓑ It's for the minibar.
這是迷你吧的費用。

舉一反三學起來！

- Could you explain this item, please?
可不可以麻煩你解釋一下這個項目？
- What's this charge for?
這筆是什麼的費用？
- I think there's a mistake here.
我想這裡有個錯誤。

關鍵字 ► explain 解釋、charge 費用、mistake 錯誤

18 免稅商店

◄◄◄ 說法比一比 ►►►

學校 **Can I pay by US dollars?**
我可以用美元付款嗎？

老外 **Do you take US dollars?**
你們收美元嗎？

 實境對話 **MP3** **166**

A Do you take US dollars?
你們收美元嗎？

B Yes, we do.
收。

舉一反三學起來！

- Can I take this on the plane?
  我可以把這個帶上飛機嗎？
- Can I take this through customs in Los Angeles?
  我可以帶這個過洛杉磯海關嗎？

關鍵字 ➤ through customs 過海關

202

後 語

　　學校沒教的英文口語其實還有很多，比如跟文化、地域、習慣、專業有關的用語和較爲不雅的俚語等，這些在學校的教科書上都很難出現。你是否也曾有過這樣的感覺：明明從小學英文學了那麼長一段時間，在國外到了一家汽車修理廠，卻無法完全用英文解釋汽車發生了什麼問題，或聽懂 mechanic（技師）對你說明車子的狀況。在美國看病，對於簡單的醫療問題或說明，是否也曾束手無策？看歐美劇集或脫口秀時，也常常跟不到笑點？甚至，在某些情形下，被罵了也渾然不知。然而，這一切都是因爲我們在學校所學習到的英文太制式，過於講究文法了。

　　在此必須重申，我們並不是要否定學校的英語教學，而是要補其不足，同時針對英文口語的適切說法給予一些提點。當然，每個人都有不同的口氣與表達方式，本書收錄的都是比較通用的，並不表示其他說法有誤，仍然有些母語人士會使用教科書裡的表達方式。不過，語言以約定俗成爲主，大家常用的就是比較適切、也是我們能溝通無礙的方式。

　　最後要強調的是，本書所列的字彙詞句，大都以美國人所使用的爲主，但和其他英文母語人士也能溝通，大家多注意電視、電影或周遭外國友人的用詞，就很容易掌握這些道地的母語表達形式。別忘了，多聽、多練習絕對是掌握語言的重要關鍵！

國家圖書館出版品預行編目（CIP）資料

學校沒教的英文口語 / David Katz作；戴至中譯. -- 二版.
　-- 臺北市：波斯納出版有限公司, 2021.08
　　面；　公分
　ISBN 978-986-06066-6-9（平裝）

　1. 英語　2. 口語　3. 會話

805.188　　　　　　　　　　　　　　　110010182

學校沒教的英文口語

作　　者／David Katz
譯　　者／戴至中
執行編輯／游玉旻

出　　版／波斯納出版有限公司
地　　址／100 台北市館前路 26 號 6 樓
電　　話／(02) 2314-2525
傳　　真／(02) 2312-3535
客服專線／(02) 2314-3535
客服信箱／btservice@betamedia.com.tw
郵撥帳號／19493777
帳戶名稱／波斯納出版有限公司

總 經 銷／時報文化出版企業股份有限公司
地　　址／桃園市龜山區萬壽路二段 351 號
電　　話／(02) 2306-6842

出版日期／2021 年 8 月二版一刷
定　　價／280 元
Ｉ Ｓ Ｂ Ｎ／978-986-06066-6-9

Ⓑ 貝塔網址：www.betamedia.com.tw

喚醒你的英文語感！

Get a Feel for English !